Steamy Espresso Secrets

Tyora Moody

Steamy Espresso Secrets
Joss Miller Mysteries, Book 4

Copyright © 2025 by Tyora Moody

Steamy Espresso Secrets is a work of fiction. Names, characters, places and incidents either are products of the author's imagination or are used fictitiously. Any resemblance to actual persons, living or dead, events, or locales is entirely coincidental.

Published by
Tymm Publishing LLC
www.tymmpublishing.com

Paperback ISBN: 978-1-961437-34-0
Ebook ISBN: 978-1-961437-33-3

Cover Design: TywebbinCreations.com
Editing: Felicia Murrell

Contents

Chapter 1
Brewing Concerns

Monday, June 2 at 10:37 a.m.

Never could I have imagined this.

Unexpected tears welled in my eyes as I took stock of the kids scattered around the classroom inside the Rebecca Montgomery Art Center. Being attacked at the café next door, this time last year, was the scariest moment of my life. But God brought me closer to my purpose. I was feeling a sense of overwhelm, but it sprung from joy rather than despair.

Before anyone noticed, I turned my head and quickly wiped the moisture from my eyes. This was the first day of our first annual media arts summer camp, and I had the honor of kicking it off with a podcasting workshop. I'd specifically requested to work with eight to eleven year olds.

The Sugar Creek Media Arts Camp was my brainchild. I thought it would be good to get kids interested in media arts at an early age. Since the art center had become a part of Sugar Creek Café, Fay loved the idea. The café had been a fixture in the arts community for years with its bimonthly Friday Night Jams. Patrons already enjoyed the paintings and photography displayed on the walls of the café, and we'd expanded the galleries in the art center to include sculptures, pottery, sweetgrass baskets and mixed-media pieces.

Watching these young minds craft their own podcast episode was more rewarding than I'd expected. I worked with a teacher to develop a curriculum that included writing, storytelling, oratory and computer skills. We were flooded with applications, but I stuck to twelve slots. With the lower age range, that wasn't hard to do.

"Okay, everyone, let's wrap up your scripts. I'm coming around to each of you. I can't wait to hear what you're going to record later this afternoon." I didn't want to hold back their creativity, but the recordings were going home for their families to hear. The last thing I wanted was an angry parent.

Eight-year-old Kisha Black spun around in her chair. "Auntie, I mean Miss Joss, I wrote about the mystery of the missing Squishmallow!"

Though we weren't related, Kisha's mom was one of my best friends, and I'd become an honorary auntie. I reached down and playfully wiggled my eyebrows at the little girl. "A mystery? You trying to give me some competition for my podcast, Kisha?"

She giggled into her hands. "You know my daddy is a detective. He's always solving mysteries. I might be like him when I grow up, or a teacher like Grandma Eugeena."

This wasn't a surprise. Kisha came from a mystery loving family. Her dad, Detective Chris Black, her mom, Leesa Patterson-Black, and my next-door neighbor, Eugeena Patterson-Jones, were true crime aficionados, the latter two were amateur sleuths like me. I was thrilled when Leesa told me how interested Kisha was in the podcasting session.

"A Squishmallow mystery?" I asked, trying to keep a straight face. Andre had gotten me one for my birthday. The purple cat lived on my bed when it wasn't getting knocked off by one of the real felines in the house. I was curious to hear Kisha's explanation.

Kisha's eyes lit up. "They're super soft stuffed animals! I have one that looks like Grandma Eugeena's dog. Anyway, my friend Emma brought her Hello Kitty one to school last week, and everyone wanted to touch it. But after lunch, when Emma went to get it from her desk, it was gone!" Kisha put her arms in the air. "We looked everywhere."

Intrigued, I asked. "Did you all ever find it?"

Her barrettes clanged as she shook her head. "No. But I have some ideas about who might have taken it. Daddy says I need to follow the clues."

I couldn't help but grin. "Alright, Detective Kisha. I'm looking forward to hearing more." I continued moving between the tables checking on each child's progress. At eleven years old, Amani Gladstone was the oldest in the group, and I could tell she'd written a detailed script. She had filled almost two pages with her curly writing. She'd drawn little hearts over the 'i's' like I did when I was younger.

"And what will your podcast be about, Amani?"

The young girl placed her hands on her hip, swinging one of her two long braids across her shoulder. "I'm going to talk about why adults say one thing but do another."

Her voice carried a slight edge that made me eye her a bit more carefully. "That's... a really interesting topic. What made you think of that?"

Amani held her finger in the air as she made her point. "Adults are always telling kids to be honest and tell the truth, but then *they* don't."

By the way she rolled her neck, I wasn't sure I wanted to go there. But it might also open up some much needed dialogue if

Amani shared her episode with her mom later. "Well, I'm sure a lot of other kids will be able to relate to your episode."

I glanced at the clock on the wall. Fifteen minutes until lunch break, then we'd record the podcast episodes this afternoon. Thanks to our camp sponsor, the local tech company, Synaptic, we had a nice setup with real microphones and recording equipment. The company's CEO also insisted we have Mac-Books loaded with their newest software.

It was the same software I used to edit my podcast. Since I found it super easy to use, I knew these young digital natives would have no issues with it. I figured all of them had their hands on a phone or tablet since they were toddlers. The biggest obstacle this morning had been getting my campers to settle on stories they wanted to record.

"Joss," My boss Fay Everett's voice drifted from the classroom doorway. "Lunch is ready. We have everything set up in the back room. I can take them over to the café for you."

"Sounds good." I clapped my hands twice. "Alright, young podcasters, it's time for lunch. This afternoon you'll get to hear your voices come through those fancy microphones."

The kids cheered as they headed toward the door. They lined up behind Fay, and I took a breath before gathering the scattered pencils and markers.

A noise near the doorway caught my attention. I spun around, expecting to see a child returning to the classroom.

Instead, I glimpsed a man standing in the hallway. He appeared familiar to me, but I couldn't recall if he was one of the campers' parents. Something about his intense stare made my skin prickle. Despite the café being next door, I suddenly felt very alone.

Monday, June 2 at 11:56 a.m.

My mind whirred to the incident that happened last June. The man who attacked me inside the café was behind bars, but from that incident, I'd learned I couldn't trust anyone. Even though the café was right next door, it seemed far away.

The stranger and I stared at one another for what felt entirely too long before I found my voice and croaked out, "Can I help you?"

The man stepped forward. "I'm sorry for disturbing you. Fay let me in. My name is Devante Cavanaugh. I'm teaching the photography class tomorrow. I wanted to see how things were going."

"Oh." My shoulders sagged with relief. That's why I recognized the man. I was the one who'd researched him online and discovered he lived right here in Charleston. He looked different in person. I cocked my head to the side and then blurted. "Didn't you have dreadlocks?"

He smiled, rubbing his hand across his low cut fade. "Yes, I parted with them a few weeks ago."

I nodded, suddenly aware that I was still clutching the basket of pencils and markers to my body. "Well, change is always good." I placed the basket on the desk at the front of the room and wiped my sweaty hands on my jeans. "Hmm... as you can see, we stuck to a young group for this first camp."

Devante's brown eyes were piercing above high cheekbones. "They seem bright and..." he tilted his head as if listening for a sound, "energetic too."

I laughed. "Yes! Food makes us all pretty excited. I promise they're a good group. Do you want to meet them? I need to catch up to them." It was great that Fay came to get the campers, but she still was managing the café too.

Devante moved out of the way as I rushed past him. Even though he'd identified himself, my discomfort quickly returned, and I wasn't sure why. He didn't appear to be a monster. In fact, he was incredibly handsome. His looks didn't make me nervous; I had a handsome boyfriend who I was head over heels in love with. Maybe it was the cologne that seemed to reach out and grab my nostrils as I passed. It was strong and spicy.

The familiar scent of freshly ground coffee soothed me as I slid through the double doors that connected to Sugar Creek Café. This time of day, I was usually serving up coffee concoctions alongside pastries and muffins. The lunch crowd wasn't quite in full swing, but I could hear our group of campers as I drew closer to the back of the café. While I couldn't see him, I could feel Devante trailing behind me.

The front of the café was set up with tables and chairs in the center and booths along the windows. Unlike some of the trendier coffeehouses, Sugar Creek Café gave off an at-home-in-your-kitchen vibe. In the back were couches and chairs for those who wanted to read or study. Last night, we'd pushed the plush chairs closer to the wall and set up tables and folding chairs in the center.

I'd asked Fay why not have the campers eat lunch inside the center, but she said, "Might as well give them the whole café experience." This was a big deal for some kids who never ventured outside of Charleston, or explored their hometown.

All twelve campers chattered as they devoured their turkey sandwiches, chips, and fresh homemade lemonade. Fay arrived early every morning to bake fresh pastries or muffins and to make gourmet sandwiches. This group would have a special treat that café patrons wouldn't get, Fay's decadent M&M chocolate chip cookies.

I was enjoying seeing the kids having such a good time. I almost forgot about Devante. I glanced back and found him standing off to the side, observing the kids. But I'd caught his eye. Out of habit, I smiled, then quickly turned away from those intense eyes. It was times like this when I wished Andre had a ring on my finger. Not that that would deter some men. Of course, I could've been reading too much into the man's intentions.

I hadn't had a ton of boyfriends in the past, but my experiences with men had made me wary. I casually looked in his direction again, but he'd moved over to the wall of photos. Fay supported the arts, including several local photographers. It occurred to me that Devante might not be among the photographers on the wall. I hoped that wasn't a problem. Most of the photographs were of places in Charleston. Devante specialized in portraits.

TYORA MOODY

The café door chimed as people arrived for the lunch hour. Though Fay said I wasn't officially on duty in the café today, familiar habits had me peeking around the corner in case I needed to jump in and help. To my surprise, my boyfriend Detective Andre Baez walked in and behind him was my brother.

"Nate?" My voice came out low, under my breath.

My brother mainly stayed missing in action since we'd lost our father. Surprisingly, he'd stayed in Sugar Creek this past Thanksgiving and into the New Year, the longest he'd been in town in years. He even came for Mother's Day three weeks ago. But why was he here now? And why was he hanging out with my boyfriend?

Andre wore one of his suits, but must have left the jacket in the car. His red tie hung slightly loose around his neck with the sleeves of his white shirt rolled up to his elbow. Next to him, my brother wore a light blue t-shirt that stretched over his biceps and jeans. On his feet were Nike sneakers that I was sure was one style among several hundred pairs. My brother had always been a sneakerhead.

I glanced over at the kids. They were chatting and finishing up their meal, so I walked over to greet Andre and Nate.

"Hey, sis." Nate grinned before giving me a one-armed hug. "Surprise."

"What are you doing here?" I asked Nate, before walking into Andre's outstretched arms. "Glad you dropped by," I murmured into his chest. "And why didn't you tell me he was coming?"

I stepped back, eyeing my brother and my boyfriend.

Andre's expression was carefully masked. I'd told him if I knew how to play poker, I would never go against him. Because of his training, he'd perfected the art of maintaining a stoic face, which also alerted me that something was up.

"I didn't know," Andre shrugged.

I tilted my head, ready to question him further.

Nate quickly interjected. "Now hold on, Sis. We ran into each other. Andre said he was going to catch lunch at Sugar Creek Café and that I could find you here."

I studied my brother's face. Mmm, right! My brother happened to run into my boyfriend. I still hadn't figured out how Andre tracked down Nate and got him to come home for the holidays, when Nate had been ignoring my texts and emails.

I wanted to know exactly where they'd ran into each other. Instead, I asked. "How long are you staying?"

Nate licked his lips. "Not sure yet. Depends on a few things."

That was pretty vague. What was he hiding?

Andre cleared his throat and pointed. "Is that your group of future podcasters in the back? Sounds like they're having fun."

"Yep, we're recording their episodes after lunch. I'm hoping to get them all recorded by the time camp ends at four o'clock. It took longer than I'd thought for them to come up with ideas."

Andre raised an eyebrow. "Do you have any help?"

"Hailey, the teacher who helped me with the curriculum, is coming to help this afternoon. She had something to do this morning." I glanced at my brother before leaning closer to Andre. "Are we getting together tonight?"

Andre grimaced and then shook his head. "They added me to a task force for a case that came up."

I stepped back, crossing my arms. "A task force? That sounds pretty serious."

He nodded. "Yeah, it involves a couple of agencies, including the Feds."

My heart sank. When Andre was on a task force a few months ago, we hardly saw each other. I crossed my arms and eyed Nate, suddenly wanting to place my frustration on my brother. "Does Mom know you're here?"

He shook his head. "Not yet. Thought I would grab some lunch for her. What does she usually like?"

I sighed. "The chicken salad croissant sandwich and an iced latte."

"Auntie Joss?"

I turned to find Kisha behind me.

She glanced over and then sprinted toward Andre. "Hey, Uncle Andre."

Andre bent down to hug the little girl. "Hey, Kisha."

"Have you seen my daddy?"

Andre grinned. "I saw Detective Black this morning. He told me you would be at camp today with Auntie Joss."

Kisha clapped her hands together. "I can't wait for him and Mommy to hear my podcast." She grabbed my hand. "Is it time for us to use the microphones yet?"

I rubbed her hand. "Almost. Do me a favor. Make sure everyone puts their trash in the big garbage can back there."

"Got it." Kisha headed back to the room.

We all laughed as we heard her repeat my instructions to the group.

"I need to grab something to eat myself." I playfully punched my brother on the arm. "I'm looking forward to finding out more about this surprise visit." Turning back to Andre, I reached up and kissed him. "I'll see you when I see you. Text me if plans change."

He smiled, "You got it, babe."

While Andre and Nate headed toward the counter to place their order, I went back to grab a sandwich and make sure the campers had cleaned up any remnants of lunch in the back room. Despite the kids' chatter around me, my mind raced. Why was Nate really here? And why did it feel like Andre knew more than he was saying?

I was so lost in thought, I'd forgotten about Devante. Maybe he had questions about the camp and his workshop tomorrow.

Feeling bad that I'd left him hanging, I looked around, prepared to apologize.

But he was gone.

Chapter 2

Grounds for Suspicion

Monday, June 2 at 4:35 p.m.

For the next few hours, I forgot about Devante Cavanaugh. I also had little time to think about my brother's sudden appearance in town. Thankfully, Hailey Ramsey, a former barista, now elementary school teacher and my curriculum coordinator, joined me as a volunteer. With another adult, the afternoon ran smoothly. Each camper received a MacBook loaded with the Synaptic editing software and headphones with a microphone. I snapped several photos of the kids hunched over their MacBooks, headsets on, looking more like mini-professionals than summer campers.

After each camper recorded their episode, Hailey and I showed them how to edit their audio track. I was grinning the whole time, watching their intense faces sporting headphones almost too big for their heads.

Kisha recapped what happened during the Great Squishmallow Mystery. She provided her theories with the serious tone of a seasoned detective detailing evidence in a case. I couldn't wait to hear Leesa and Chris's reaction.

Amani's episode about adults saying one thing and doing another was insightful for an eleven-year-old. She'd cited specific examples that proved her point, and I hoped Amani's mom would keep an open mind when she heard the recording.

I felt elated that the first day of camp had gone well. By the time three-thirty arrived, exhaustion had settled in. I made a mental note to send Synaptic a thank you for providing the equipment. Everything went off without a hitch, even down to transferring the mp3 files to individual flash drives for each camper. Each flash drive was customized with *Sugar Creek Media Arts Camp* printed in bold block letters. There were a rainbow of primary colors to choose from, but Hailey used the classroom label maker to make sure no one grabbed the wrong one.

Amani's grandmother, Rosemary Gladstone, arrived first to pick up her granddaughter. I didn't need to warn her grandmother. Amani took care of that herself.

"I recorded a podcast about the way adults act sometimes. I hope Mom will listen."

Rosemary raised an eyebrow at me. "Oh, I'm sure your mother will listen. Sounds like you had a good time today."

Amani nodded, "Yes, I want to do this again." She turned to me. "I have a laptop, and I'd like to use that software and get my own tiny mic."

I had to suppress my grin as my heart swelled with pride. "Inside your folder is some more information about the equipment and software we used today. Synaptic provided a discount for participating in the camp."

Detective Chris Black arrived as Amani and her grandmother exited through the front door. Chris worked alongside Andre, and I noticed despite the warm temperatures, the two detectives sported the same dress code. A white dress shirt with rolled up sleeves, a tie, and slacks.

Kisha rushed over to Chris, and he bent down to hug her. She exclaimed, "Guess what? I did a mystery podcast like Auntie Joss."

Chris glanced over at me before turning his attention back to his daughter. "Okay, I see the adults have rubbed off on you. I can't wait to hear this mystery you recorded."

I chuckled. "She did a great job. And you will be proud of how she laid out her logic and the clues."

After everyone left, we cleaned off the tables and secured the equipment inside a metal cabinet in the storage room. Hailey leaned against the doorframe while I locked up. "That was a lot of fun today. I really appreciate you inviting me to assist."

I stuck the keys in my jeans pocket and headed back toward the classroom. "I'm glad you could help. After your first year of teaching, I'm surprised you wanted to be around kids during the summer."

Hailey laughed as she trailed behind me. "Me too. I definitely had some rough moments during my first year. But I love kids, and you had a great group today. What's going on the rest of the week?"

I pointed to a box in the classroom's corner. "Well, tomorrow is the photography session. We have some kiddie phones that are equipped with a camera and are already loaded with age appropriate photography apps." I handed her a copy of the itinerary I'd typed up for the week. "Are you planning on coming any other days this week?"

Hailey scanned the schedule. "Wow! This is great, Joss. And yes, I'd absolutely love to come. I see Devante Cavanaugh is leading tomorrow's photography session."

I glanced over at her. "You know him?"

Hailey shrugged. "Not personally. He was the photographer for my sister's wedding last fall. The photos turned out great. He's creative," she pushed her glasses up her nose as redness crept up around her cheeks, "and also really good looking."

I laughed lightly, remembering how intense the man looked at me earlier today. I couldn't argue with that assessment.

"Well, we could certainly use an extra hand, especially when we head outside. Devante added a few spots around the business district to the itinerary for some camera shots."

Hailey grinned. "That sounds so cool! The weather should be good tomorrow too. Do you need anything else from me? If not, I will see you in the morning."

"I'm good. But let's leave through the café, I've already locked the center's main entrance."

After we entered the café, I secured the double doors.

Hailey waved goodbye and headed out the café entrance.

"Have a good evening," I said, glancing at the clock. There was still over an hour left before the café closed. One of our newest baristas was wiping down the countertop.

"What's up, Ace? How are classes going?"

Ace Clark looked up and smiled. "Not bad. I heard today went well with the camp. I wish that kind of camp existed when I was younger. What's going on tomorrow?"

Before I mentioned it, it occurred to me that Ace would've been perfect for tomorrow's session. "We've got Devante Cavanaugh coming in to teach photography, but you probably could have done it too." I paused. Ace's expression had shifted slightly. "I'm sorry for not asking, Ace. You seemed pretty busy with work and school." In addition to school and working here in the café, Ace was also still helping his mom out at the insurance company across the street.

Ace gave me a small smile and continued to wipe the counter. "You're right, Joss. I am too busy right now, but I'm not so sure if Devante is the best person."

Uh oh! Just when I was feeling good about Devante from my conversation with Hailey, Ace burst my bubble.

My earlier reservations crept back.

I had a habit of doubting my own instincts. But then again, I was the one who found Devante's social media and invited him. I could tell he was a brilliant photographer from the posts on his social media feed. His work spoke for itself with portraits ranging from newlyweds to business professionals, families to babies. He'd even posted behind-the-scenes videos, putting his subjects at ease before taking their photographs.

The in-person meeting earlier today disturbed me, and I still wasn't sure why. I hoped this would not be a horrible lesson in trusting social media profiles. I'd been burned by someone on social media before. My attacker last year was not who he portrayed himself to be on social media. I cleared my throat. "So, you know him?"

Ace tossed the rag into the sanitizer bucket. "Devante was a few years ahead of me in school. He wasn't really nice to me, and he's not who he pretends to be now."

I went to school in a different county, but Leesa told me Ace had a rough time with bullies. I leaned against the counter, not wanting to upset him, but I had to know more. "What do you mean? You don't think people can change?"

Ace glanced around. Fay was probably in the office, but he seemed to not want to be overheard. "I believe people can change. But I also think people can give the illusion that they have changed." He tilted his head. "You heard about Lens? That's his sobriquet."

"Sobr—" I frowned. "What?"

Ace blushed. "Sorry! That's a word from my spelling bee days. It means nickname. His real name was Jerome McAbee."

I chuckled. "Okay. Expanding my vocabulary." Ace had been a spelling bee champion when he was younger. The reason for his nickname or whatever word he said. I couldn't say it, so I knew I couldn't spell it either. I racked my brain for a few seconds on the name. "Lens? That name sounds familiar. I follow a lot of profiles online. Is he from around here?"

"Yeah, Lens, that's what I called him, was from Charleston." Ace's jaw tightened. "He was a good friend, and he always had my back. Lens taught me how to use a DSLR camera. He cared about this city, about showing people what was actually happening behind the scenes."

I turned my head toward the back of the café. Fay had some of Ace's photos on the wall. There were quite a few artists in the café that I didn't know or had never met. "So are his photos the black and white ones on the other side of yours?"

Ace nodded. "Yeah, that was his favorite style. He took photos of people. Like all kinds of people. People who are often overlooked like the homeless, poor people, kids playing, older people. He had a way of finding beauty or good in everything."

I crossed my arms, suddenly feeling a chill. "You're speaking about him in past tense."

Ace cleared his throat. He attempted to speak but his voice came out hoarse, as if he had an obstruction in his throat. "That's because he's dead."

I reached my hand toward him. "I'm so sorry. I hate to ask, but what happened to him?"

Ace turned away from me. "Cops say he drowned. But no one believed that! Definitely not me. I know for a fact that Lens couldn't stand being near deep water."

I came around the counter so I could stand next to Ace. "You don't think Lens's death was accidental?"

Ace was quiet for a long moment, organizing the cups that were already perfectly organized. "No, I don't. His family doesn't believe it either. The cops claimed he 'slipped and drowned' near the port." He turned to face me, his eyes brimming with tears. "Something happened to him. Somebody got to him. His camera and backpack disappeared. He carried those everywhere with him."

My mind buzzed with this information. "How long ago was this?"

Ace took a deep breath. "Hard to believe, but it's been almost two years this month."

"Oh my! I'm sure you really miss Lens."

Ace lost his father a year ago. Since then, he'd become a regular at the café and we'd bonded over losing our dads. He mentioned he was looking for another job, and I'd encouraged him to apply to the café.

Earlier today, Devante was looking at the wall of photos. Had he recognized Lens's work? "How does this involve Devante? Were he and Lens friends?"

Ace rolled his eyes. "Cousins, but not close. I feel like Devante has tried to capitalize on Lens's social media following since he's been gone."

My eyebrows shot up in surprise. "Capitalize. How?"

Ace crossed his arms. "He's always talking about 'honoring Lens's legacy' and all that. When Lens was alive, Devante looked down on Lens's form of photography. To me, Lens created art. Devante is more into what he can get paid."

I nodded. "Yeah, I can see that since he's into more commercial photography. Both are talented in different ways. Maybe Devante now sees that he'd been unfair to Lens."

Ace didn't appear to be convinced by my suggestion so I changed the subject. "So, do you have any theories about what happened to him?"

Ace bit his lip and looked behind him again. Fay hadn't come out of her office, but Ace seemed to want this conversation to be between us. "Lens was working on something big before he died, but he wouldn't tell me about it."

A chill ran down my spine. "You think it's what got him killed?"

Ace gulped. "Yeah, I do."

"Did you talk to the cops at all?"

Ace grimaced. "No one came to talk to me. Besides, it's not like I have proof. But I felt like Lens was being extra about something that last week."

"Extra? Like excited or scared?"

Ace thought for a moment. "Maybe both? Like he'd discovered something, but wasn't ready to let the lid off it yet."

"Do you know who else Lens talked to?"

Ace hesitated. "Everybody. He posted he had something big in the works on Instagram. It was his last post."

My eyes widened. I'd been working hard on launching the *Cold Justice Podcast* that summer. I must have been so immersed in the premiere season about my grandfathers's legacy I'd missed Lens's death. Or if I'd only known him from social media, I might not have realized he stopped posting. There was no way I couldn't investigate this more.

Monday, June 2 at 7:05 p.m.

Since Ace was scheduled to help Fay close up, I said my goodbyes for the evening and headed home. I wasn't sure what to think about Devante Cavanaugh from the two different perspectives Hailey and Ace provided. Tomorrow I'd watch him with the kids and see for myself what kind of person he really was. I prayed I hadn't made a mistake.

When I arrived at my grandmother's house, I opened the door to find her in her usual spot in the living room, watching her favorite game show. She appeared surprised to see me.

"Joss, honey. I thought you would be over at Andre's tonight."

I joked, "You're trying to get rid of me." I'd been staying with my grandmother for over two years now.

She laughed. "You know how much I enjoy you being here. But you also have a handsome young man. I imagine one of these days he's going to pop the question."

I wish!

After dating for over a year, Andre remained the perfect gentleman, moving more slowly than I'd expected. But he was also a cop. There were times like tonight when Andre's job took precedence over our relationship.

"Andre got assigned to some task force, so I'm here tonight."

"Well, let me get you something to eat." She moved closer to the edge of the seat. The orange cat beside her eyed me. I'd disrupted his sleep.

"No, no. You don't need to do that." I held up a brown bag labeled Sugar Creek Café. "I actually have some sandwiches and muffins. I know how much you like the banana nut bread."

I put the food on the kitchen table and went to my room to change my clothes. After getting cleaned up a bit and putting on a big t-shirt I'd nicked from Andre, I headed back down the stairs.

I curled up on the couch with my laptop. One of the twin tuxedo cats, Minnie, settled beside me, purring softly. I chatted with my grandmother, sharing everything about my day from the campers to my brother's surprise visit.

Louise reassured me. "I'm sure your mother is glad that your brother is home. Maybe he realized how much he missed you all after spending so much time here during the holidays."

"You think so?" I was usually an optimistic person, but my brother had made it a point to be out of our lives for so long, I felt nothing but suspicion. It wasn't like he'd ever explained his absence, at least not to me. My mother and brother had a totally different relationship. Growing up, I was a daddy's girl, and Nate was a mama's boy. Even with him not being around, my mother seemed more sympathetic toward him.

"He's finding his way."

I thought I was trying to do the same thing, but I continued to receive criticism for my efforts.

My grandmother scooted toward the end of the chair, and with some effort, she rose. "Well, dear. I'm glad you're here tonight, but I'm afraid I need to get some shut-eye."

"Good night, Louise!" I watched as she moved slowly down the hallway. Since coming to stay with her, my grandmother didn't do the stairs much. When she moved back into her home after a brief stint in the nursing home, she'd turned what used to be a guest bedroom into her primary bedroom on the first level. While I enjoyed staying over at Andre's, I worried about my grandmother. Besides me, she didn't have anyone else.

As an adoptee, my mother had a complicated family history. Her relationship with her biological mother had improved, but I wasn't sure what would happen to Louise if I ever moved out.

Once Louise's door closed behind her, I returned to my MacBook. Since my conversation with Ace, I couldn't stop thinking about Lens. Before leaving the café, I'd looked at the wall of photos again and recognized the style. I knew I had to be following his Instagram account.

I searched for "Jerome Lens McAbee Charleston photographer." Once the Instagram account popped up at the top of the results, I clicked on it.

@BehindtheLensATL Street Photographer | Charleston, SC | Capturing the real stories behind the mask

I found it fascinating that Lens had been dead for almost two years, but his legacy continued to live on this platform. His face looked familiar, but I was sure I'd never met him in person. Social media was like that sometimes. The algorithm displayed people to you so often, you almost felt like you knew them. I wondered if the ATL part of his handle had anything to do with Atlanta. Charleston was listed as his location in his profile.

I studied his profile photo. Like Devante, he wore his hair in a low cut fade, but the top of his was bleached blond. Slanted brown eyes peered back at me, charming and alive. Like many of his peers, Lens also used his body as a canvas. Colorful tattoos covered his caramel arms and even around his neck. In his profile photo, he wore small gold hoops in his ears and had a nose piercing. His bright smile was warm and inviting.

Before diving into a specific post, I scrolled through his profile feed. The photos were stunning. Black and white images that captured the soul of Charleston in ways I'd never seen before. There were candid shots of kids playing in sprinklers on hot summer days, an older Black man and White man playing chess, a street musician playing his guitar, and so many other captivating images. Each photo told a story; I scrolled for nearly thirty minutes. Lens had been so talented.

I'd intentionally not played any reels, but now I was curious. I returned to the top of his profile feed and clicked on the last reel before his death.

@BehindtheLensATL: *Hey, y'all, thanks for coming with me on this journey today. Let's see who I can get on camera today."*

I noticed Lens passed several people as if they weren't interesting enough to him. Then, he stopped in front of a homeless man sitting outside a downtown shop.

@BehindtheLensATL: *"Mind if I take your picture? I'd like to show people your story."*

The man looked at him, his eyes wary. Lens pulled out some bills and handed them to the man, whose eyes filled with tears of gratitude.

Lens took several shots of the man, who grinned a toothless smile. At the end of the shoot, Lens took the man into a restaurant to get something to eat. Before the video ended, Lens had edited the results of the photoshoot.

Each angle that captured the man's weathered, dark skin blew me away. I could tell the man had probably been handsome at one time, but life had dealt him a blow. And I loved the caption. **@BehindtheLensATL:** *Every wrinkle is a chapter. Every smile is a victory.*

The next reel showed Lens talking to a young street artist spray painting a mural.

@BehindtheLensATL: *This is beautiful, man. Can I document your process?*

The artist nodded, *"Sure, man."*

Lens filmed the artist explaining his technique and his inspiration. The shoot must have taken a few days because Lens captured the artist with different clothes on. Toward the end of the reel, the film speeded up to show the full mural depicting children of all ages playing jump rope and hopscotch.

There was something special about the way Lens connected with people. He didn't just take their pictures, he saw them, respected them, and gave them a voice. Once again, I had the thought: *I wished I had known him.*

Remembering what Ace said, I went back to the last post. It wasn't a black-and-white photo, but a selfie. That alone was different; most of the photos and reel thumbnails were of other people. The only photo of Lens had been his profile photo. He didn't seem to be the selfie type.

Up close, I could see the tattoo on his left bicep was a camera silhouette. A filmstrip flowed from it like a dark serpent, winding down his forearm and coiling around his wrist. Each individual frame in the filmstrip contained tiny images. I could make out what looked like a lightning bolt in one of the first frames. Lens's body was another whole masterpiece to explore, but my eyes were pulled to the last caption.

@BehindtheLensATL: *The lens reveals what the heart refuses to see.*

Wow! What had Lens captured with his camera?

My ringing phone startled me as I tried to study some of the smaller imagery. I peeked over and saw Andre's name on the screen.

"Hey," I answered, grateful to hear his voice after the long day.

"Sorry about tonight," he said; exhaustion filled his voice. "This task force has a lot of agencies involved, so egos were high. How was your day? How'd the camp go?"

"The kids were amazing." I paused before deciding to dive in. "Andre, do you remember a case from two years ago? A photographer named Jerome McAbee, but he went by Lens, supposedly drowned near the port."

There was a long beat of silence on the other end, then Andre said. "That's kind of random. Why are you asking about that?"

"Well, I was talking to Ace after finishing up with the camp. He and Lens were friends, and he doesn't think Lens's death was an accident."

Andre sighed. "I was still pretty new then. But I remember hearing about it around the station."

"What did you hear?"

"Officially? Accidental drowning. Guy was out taking photos late at night, slipped and fell in. His body was found the next morning." Andre's voice took on that careful tone he used when he was walking the line between sharing information and protecting an investigation. "But..."

"But what?"

"I heard Detective Wilkes thought there were some things that didn't add up. The guy's camera equipment was never recovered, which was strange. That stuff usually floats or washes up eventually."

Ace had mentioned that. "Is there any other information you can get for me?"

"Joss." Andre's voice held a warning. "That's Detective Wilkes's case. You know how she is about her cases."

I was quite familiar with Detective Sarah Wilkes. She'd interrogated me regarding two different homicide cases. The woman was relentless but also admired in the department for her close rate. If this was one of her cases, it sounded like she didn't think it was really open and shut.

Andre had been talking while my mind floated elsewhere. "Besides, you started the camp. Don't you think you should focus on that instead of diving into another cold case?"

"I'm curious." My voice sounded a bit too high in my ears, which made me sound more defensive than I intended.

"Uh-huh. I know where this is going. I also know it's been awhile since you had a *Cold Justice Podcast* season, and you're always searching for the next case."

This man knew me too well!

"How do you know?"

"I know you, Joss Miller. Sometimes I think you make a better detective than me." I couldn't see his face, but I could sense his smile.

I was grinning too, but then I sobered when I looked back at my laptop screen at Lens's last post.

"Andre, what if someone killed him because of something he photographed? What if there's evidence out there that could help his family get answers?"

I waited through another long pause, then Andre said, "The last thing we both need is for Detective Wilkes to find out you're sniffing around one of her cases. And I shouldn't have to remind you, if this guy really was murdered, whoever did it is still out there."

"I know, I know. It's not like I'm dropping a podcast episode tomorrow," I joked.

But we both knew my track record when I pursued a case for the *Cold Justice Podcast*. So far, my persistence had brought justice and more trouble than I needed in my life.

"Love you, Joss. I hope camp goes well tomorrow."

"Thanks, Andre. I love you too. Get some sleep, okay? You sound exhausted, Bae."

After he hung up, I stared at Lens's Instagram post for a long time, studying his last photo for clues. If Lens died because he'd captured something he shouldn't have, then his story deserved to be told.

What did you see, Lens?

Chapter 3

Steamy Surprises

Tuesday, June 3 at 7:11 a.m.

Despite my late night investigating Lens's online presence, I arrived early to Sugar Creek Café. We kept the front entrance locked until the café officially opened, so I pulled out my key and entered. Fay was in the back, bustling around the oven. The clang of pans and gospel music greeted me as I entered the kitchen doorway.

"Good morning, Boss!" I called out on my way to my locker.

Fay looked up, her new red cat-eye glasses sat on the edge of her nose. "Good morning to you, Sunshine. You ready for the second day of camp?"

"Yes. Today should be different with someone else facilitating the workshop." I pushed my bag inside the locker and almost reached for my uniform apron before realizing I didn't need it. Instead, I grabbed the keys to the center and my phone from my bag. To keep my hands free, I stuffed the keys in the front pocket and my phone in the back pocket of my jeans. I held up my hands. "See, I'm ready! I feel like I'm babysitting today."

Fay laughed. "You have quite the crew. I listened to them talk at lunch yesterday. I hope I get to listen to those podcast episodes."

"Don't worry, I have copies. I'll share the links later today. I would have last night, but I got caught up in something else."

Fay teased. "Caught up in something? Would that be your handsome detective?"

I pouted. "I wish. He got put on some task force. I don't even know what it's about, but he was tied up last night."

I ventured closer, watching with admiration as Fay added icing to some red velvet cupcakes. Not only was my boss a coffee shop owner, she had impressive pastry chef credentials. "Mmm, those look good. They're not going to last long once the lunch crowd sees them."

Fay smiled. "I made extra. Now don't leave me hanging. What had your attention last night?"

"A case for *Cold Justice Podcast*. Well, not yet, but it's interesting. I'm sure you remember the guy. Some of his photography is on the wall in the back. Jerome "Lens" McAbee?"

Fay looked up, her face troubled. "Lens?" She slowly placed the piping bag on the counter and wiped her hands on her apron. "I haven't heard that name in quite some time. He was so talented and vibrant."

"You knew him?"

Fay tilted her head. "I knew of him. His mother attends Greater Zion Church."

"I followed him online. I'm ashamed to say, I must have been so involved in launching the first season of *Cold Justice Podcast*, I missed what happened to him."

Fay walked over to the sink to wash her hands. She grabbed a paper towel to dry them. "Yes, that was during the same time. To be honest, it happened so fast. The police said he drowned, and the family had the funeral a few days later. Really a shame." She headed back to the prep table. "I know you're not on the clock today, but can you help me get the coffee started while I set these in the display case?"

"Sure."

While Fay headed up front, I went into the storage and pulled out large coffee filters and a bag of coffee beans. Once I finished grinding the beans, I set up the two big coffee pots to brew. "What do you think happened?"

Fay had carefully lined the cupcakes inside the pastry display case. "I really don't know. Something about the whole thing didn't seem right. Lens was so young and at the top of his craft. And he had a large social media following. We're talking over a hundred thousand. "

"How did you get some of his photos on the wall in the back?"

Fay sighed. "His mother. A few weeks after his funeral, she came into the café and asked if I could hang up some of his photos. It was the least I could do to draw attention to his work. I wish he was still around. I loved the way he captured parts of Charleston that you don't often see in the magazines."

Fay took the empty pan and headed back into the kitchen.

I followed her, my mind on our conversation, but also longing for a cup of java. The rich aromas were tantalizing. "I hope things work out with Devante this morning."

Fay pulled out lettuce from the fridge. "I know Devante; he grew up at Greater Zion. And he has academic training. You know he went to Savannah College of Art and Design."

"Yeah, I saw on his resume that he attended SCAD. I guess that's good. We can let the students know how they can go to school and possibly have a career in the field."

"Absolutely." Fay peered at me over her glasses. "You have some reservations about Devante? Why?"

I sighed. "Nothing in particular. He came by yesterday to see how things were going at the camp. He kind of unnerved me. And then I heard some things about him. Like, he didn't get along with Lens."

Fay raised an eyebrow. "They were family. You know we don't always get along with people because we're related. But Devante's work speaks for itself, like Lens's did. I'm sure everything will be fine today." Fay glanced up at the clock. "Ace will arrive soon if you want to get things set up in the center. I have some fresh fruit and yogurt parfaits this morning for your campers."

"That sounds delicious. Thank you, Fay. You always know how to calm my anxiety."

I headed toward the center. After unlocking the double doors, I stuffed the keys back in my jeans pocket. The center was quiet and almost too dark in certain corners. The only light came from the sun peeking through the large windows at the entrance. I ran my hand along the wall, grateful to find the light switch.

It didn't take long to set up the classroom. Each desk held a disposable camera, phone, pencils, and paper. I glanced at the wall clock hoping I might have time to get a cup of coffee before the campers started filing in.

A knock at the entrance stopped me. Could it be a parent trying to drop their kid off early? I groaned as I trudged over to the door, still pining for coffee. It wasn't a camper; it was Devante. It made sense that he might want to arrive early. I should have thought of that.

I opened the door to greet him and stopped.

Devante wasn't alone.

Tuesday, June 3 at 8:24 a.m.

Baffled by the woman standing next to Devante, I stared. She was extraordinarily beautiful, like some supermodel stepping off a runaway. Tall and willowy, with glowing dark skin and long black silky hair pulled back in a neat ponytail, she wore a flowing maxi dress in deep purple. For this time of morning, she looked effortlessly elegant compared to the Lauren Hill t-shirt I had thrown on over my brown cargo pants. I'd dressed to be around kids.

Why was she here?

Maya McAbee's large, expressive brown eyes bore into me, sparking flashes of memory from my past. Too stunned to even say good morning, I stood there until Devante cleared his throat.

"Sorry, I should have mentioned I was bringing an assistant. I hope that's okay."

"Um, yeah, sure." Though I heard Devante say assistant, my confused mind kept falling back to one thought.

Why was my brother's ex-girlfriend here?

"Joss?" The woman's voice sounded huskier than I remembered. "It's good to see you."

"Maya. It's been a while." I wanted to add since you broke my brother's heart, but that wasn't relevant right now. In my heart, I felt like the combination of our father's death and Nate's breakup with Maya sent him over the edge, cutting me and Mom out of his life until recently. I knew little about Nate's life now, but I remembered how he adored this woman.

"You two know each other?" Devante appeared surprised as he stared at Maya through narrowed eyes.

Conscious of the tension pinging between us all, I opened the door wider. "Won't you come in? Devante, I know you need time to prepare."

After they both stepped inside, I closed the door, grateful for the wide open space of the lobby area.

Maya glanced around. "This is beautiful. I've always wanted to stop in here. I didn't know Rebecca Montgomery, but I admired her work. I'm happy y'all opened this center in her memory."

I glanced toward Rebecca's portrait which hung on the wall inside the entrance. "Yes, we've had an amazing year since opening the center. I'm glad both of you could join us for our first annual camp. Would you like anything? The café has freshly brewed coffee and breakfast pastries."

Devante smiled, but his intense eyes appeared troubled. "I've had enough coffee for today. I'd like to get to the classroom."

"Of course. Follow me." I glanced back at Maya, who dawdled to examine the current exhibit. Fay changed out the exhibits quarterly. The added space in the center allowed her to expand the artwork already on display in the café. This month, various paintings from one of our café regulars, Claude McKnight, along with two other local artists, were being featured. The exhibit showcased Charleston in the summer.

I especially liked Claude's portrait of a woman at the City Market selling sweetgrass baskets. The basketmaker's dark eyes conveyed wisdom while her hands appeared to be in motion, weaving stories as ancient as the craft itself. The earth tones made the painting feel vibrant and warm, as if summer heat radiated from the canvas.

Maya stood mesmerized in front of the portrait like she was being drawn into the woman's world. Still struggling with Maya's presence, I quickly guided Devante toward the classroom area in the back. "I wasn't sure if you wanted all the cameras available, but everything is ready to go."

Devante crossed his arms and studied the setup. "I think this is fine. I mainly wanted to show them how technology has changed over the years. I will take the disposable cameras and get the film developed so the students will have the physical photos."

I smiled. "That's pretty nice of you. We're sending all the campers's work home with them so we can store any of their digital photos on a flash drive."

He grinned. "Happy to be a part of this. So when do the campers arrive?"

I glanced at the clock on the wall. "In about twenty minutes. Once the children arrive, I'll take them into the café to get some breakfast." I thought about Devante's visit yesterday. "Do you have questions for me? I'm sorry yesterday got pretty hectic at lunchtime."

He looked at me with those intense eyes of his. I wasn't sure if he was nervous, but the man suddenly appeared like the weight of the world was on his shoulders. "No, I don't have any questions about the workshop. I am excited about working with the kids." He gazed past me, his eyes focused on something behind me.

"Okay." Curious at what had his attention, I turned to find Maya standing in the doorway. She exchanged a look with Devante that I couldn't read. But I could feel tension radiating from both of them. "Well, I'm going to head up front to greet the campers. Come inside the café and grab coffee or food if you'd like. It's on the house."

As I headed toward the door, Maya stepped back into the hallway. "How's your brother doing, Joss?"

I halted my steps, wondering why she would care. "He's in town, but I haven't caught up with him yet."

Maya's eyes widened. "Oh, I didn't know he was in Charleston."

I could feel my eyebrow raise. "You still talk to each other?"

She chuckled. "I know your recollection of me and your brother probably isn't good. We used to fight and break up, then get back together so much. But, yeah, we've been in touch."

The sound of car doors slamming outside made me glance toward the front. Parents were arriving with their kids. "I'm sure he's at our mom's house. He didn't tell me how long he would be in town. Sorry, it looks like some kids are here. I need to greet them."

My brother's love life wasn't any of my business. And what was that between Maya and Devante? Was Maya really here to help with the camp?

Tuesday, June 3 at 9:30 a.m.

I didn't have time to think about anything else as Kisha burst through the doors with Chris trailing behind her.

"Miss Joss! Are we going to play with cameras today?" Kisha asked.

I bent down as the little girl wrapped her arms around me for a hug. "Yes. Today, we're going to be photographers. But first, let's get something to eat." I looked up at Chris. "Did you want something as well?"

"I think I'll grab some coffee. This little one was up at 5:00 a.m., ready to go to camp. Her little brother wasn't too happy he couldn't come."

I pursed my lips. "Oh no. This is our first camp, so we wanted to keep it small. But Fay and I are looking into art activities we can do with preschoolers."

Chris grinned. "Sounds good."

As more kids and parents began arriving, I juggled talking to parents and getting the kids settled for breakfast inside the café. Hailey arrived as the chaos reached its peak, looking frazzled.

"Sorry I'm late," Hailey's eyes widened behind her oval glasses as she examined the room. "Oh my, this group is already bouncing off the wall."

I chuckled. "They're excited. And here I thought podcasting would be their favorite workshop. We'll wrap up breakfast in a few minutes. You should grab some coffee and food."

Hailey placed her hands under the hand sanitizer on the table and then rubbed her hands together. "Yea, well, I'm excited about today's teacher too," she added breathlessly.

I looked over to where Devante stood talking to two campers, hoping he wouldn't freak out from Hailey's starry-eyed gaze. "Girl, get a grip!" With his looks, the attention was probably normal and might not faze him.

He held a large coffee in his hand while listening intently to the kids, who were already peppering him with questions. I was pleased to see him developing a rapport with the kids. In light of how at ease he appeared, my doubts about him seemed silly.

I searched the room for Maya. Her presence still struck me as odd. I wasn't sure if it was her history with my brother or the fact that I hadn't seen her in years. Whatever her relationship with Devante, I wasn't buying the assistant story. She stood with her back to the group, her focus on the wall of photos. I hoped she was going to actually help with the kids.

I returned my attention to Hailey, who'd grabbed a coffee. "Devante brought someone with him, but I still need your help."

Hailey stepped up closer to me. "I saw that, but she doesn't look interested at all. Are they together? I mean like a couple?"

I shrugged. "I really don't know."

Hailey squinted. "He looks different from the last time I saw him at my sister's wedding."

"The locs are gone."

"Oh, that's it." She pushed her glasses up her nose. "Either way, I like how he looks." Her flushed cheeks reddened even more. "At least he's not wearing a wedding ring, so maybe he's available."

I shook my head. This girl had it bad. I needed Hailey to keep her eyes focused on the kids.

It took some wrangling from all the adults to get the kids inside the classroom. But I had to give Devante credit. He was a natural with the children and didn't seem to mind responding to zillions of questions.

"Photography is about seeing the world differently," Devante explained to the group. "It's not about pointing and clicking. It's about finding the story in everyday moments."

Devante had them practice with holding the phone cameras steady, getting close to their subjects instead of standing far away, and looking for interesting patterns in the world around them. He even showed them how to crouch down low for better angles and reminded them to keep their fingers away from the lens. That advice seemed to go in one ear and out the other with the younger kids.

It became obvious these digital babies preferred the phones. Many of them probably already had experience holding one since birth. Before long, the campers were practicing taking selfies, holding up their little fingers in poses like they were social media stars.

Devante gave photo assignments called "Your Town." "Remember, make each one tell a story about what you see."

The campers could take pictures of interesting buildings, signs, people at work, or anything that made them feel good about being a resident of Sugar Creek. We ventured outside the center, splitting the group of twelve campers into four separate groups. Hailey and I took the younger ones. Kisha stayed close by my side. Maya didn't seem too enthusiastic about the younger kids, but stuck close to our oldest campers with Amani chattering in her ear. We made it back inside the center in time for lunch.

Fay greeted the campers inside the café, serving up peanut butter and jelly on thick slices of bread. Keeping it healthy, she'd added a fruit cup of grapes, sliced strawberries, cantaloupe, and watermelon.

I noticed Maya had gone back over to the wall of photos again. My curiosity was piqued when I saw her standing in front of the black and white photos taken by Lens. I strode over beside her. "Are you a fan of his work?"

Maya glanced at me. There were tears in her eyes.

Alarmed, I glanced back at the campers. They were chatting excitedly about their morning while gobbling up their lunch. Hoping none of them noticed Maya's distress, I touched her arm. "Are you okay?"

Maya shook her head before reaching into her bag. She pulled out a Kleenex and delicately blotted her long eyelashes. With some effort, she contained her tears while still managing to look pretty. I admired women who could avoid the ugly cry look. That was a skill I didn't possess.

She composed herself and offered me her full attention. "I really need your help, Joss."

I'd been wondering why Maya was really here. But how did she think I could help?

Chapter 4

Bubbling Tension

Tuesday, June 3 at 2:44 p.m.

Maya disappeared after her plea for help. Devante didn't seem to care that his assistant was missing. I guess she hadn't really been much help most of the day. Still, I wondered what her true intentions were. Had she only shown up to ask for my help?

But for what? What could she need my help for?

Devante jumped right into the photo editing session. Already an avid subscriber of Synaptic's audio software, I'd recently started using their newest software to create graphics for social media, so I was pretty familiar with it. Devante showed the campers how to retrieve and edit their morning photos from our neighborhood field trip.

The campers observed his movements on the big screen as he explained the basic tenets of editing. "See how we can adjust the brightness here? You can also crop the image to focus on what's most important."

The software offered frames and templates for the kids to create electronic scrapbooks. But it didn't take the kids long to learn, which wasn't surprising.

While the kids edited away, Hailey and I set up the final activity. I was sure it would be popular. Each camper would get their own selfie stick fitted with a phone. We were adding ring lights to three select locations around the center for them to take selfies.

Hailey set up the third ring light in front of a group of paintings. "This is so exciting."

I grinned. "I know, right! I'm looking forward to seeing the poses from our little group."

Something caught my attention outside the front window. I spotted Maya in front of the center, talking with a tall, dark-skinned man in a white baseball cap. Even from a distance, something about his posture seemed familiar.

He turned slightly, and I recognized the sculpted profile of Tre Kennedy, the spoken word artist performing later this week at Friday Night Jam. I'd created social media graphics for this weekend that included his picture. Opening the arts center had allowed us to recruit more acts.

Maya peered up into Tre's face and he leaned down to kiss her.

Oh, okay! PDA.

Andre and I had been guilty of public displays of affection as well, but I still felt like I'd caught Maya and Tre in some crazy act.

I turned away and headed down the hall to grab the roll of carpet from the corner. When I saw it online, I thought the long hallway runner would create the perfect red carpet moment. I unrolled the carpet in front of the center's signature mural. Fay and I had painted stacks of colorful books to form a tree trunk. We'd been so pleased with the mural that a smaller version had become the center's official logo.

Behind me, I heard the double doors swing open. I turned expecting to see Fay peeking in from the café. But it wasn't.

Maya had returned.

Did she really need to be here?

My face must have showed what I was thinking. She sputtered. "I'm so sorry. I had to take care of something. Oh, and I have someone who wanted to say hello."

Tre stepped inside the center. "Hey, what's up, Joss?"

I smiled. "Hey, Tre. It's good to see you. Thank you so much for participating in Friday Night Jam. You will be a part of a great lineup."

Tre nodded. "Looking forward to it. I will have something special for the crowd."

Maya spun around, looking at our decorations. "My, my. It looks like opening night for a movie premiere."

"Thank you, Maya. We had fun pulling this all together." I paused, unsure if I should ask or not. If Maya was going to be hanging around, she might as well be useful. "Do you want to help us pass out these selfie sticks?"

Maya reached out her hand. "Oh, how cute! This is something I can help with for sure."

I didn't doubt it. It was approaching three in the afternoon, and Maya still looked as pulled together as she did this morning.

As I suspected, the campers didn't need any help posing with their selfie sticks. I got a kick out of observing the kids pose individually and with each other.

Out of the corner of my eye, I noticed Devante, Maya, and Tre huddled in the corner. The three of them formed a tight triangle, their voices low but their body language tense. Devante kept shaking his head, while Maya stabbed her fingers in

Devante's direction. Tre stood between them, his hands raised like he was trying to mediate.

I didn't want these folks to spoil anything for the kids, so I sauntered over to them. They all stopped talking abruptly when they saw me.

"Everything okay over here?"

Tre spoke first, his voice smooth. "Everything is cool. Right, Devante?" He placed a hand on Devante's shoulder.

Devante flinched. A flash of anger crossed his face as he shrugged away Tre's touch. He cleared his throat, attempting to smile. He gestured toward the kids as they chattered with their selfie sticks. "This part may be more fun than my session."

I was deeply concerned about the tension radiating off these adults, but I forced a smile. "I'm sure the campers had a great time today."

Maya stepped forward. "Joss, when do you think we can talk?"

"Maya—" Devante's voice carried a warning.

Maya shot him a look that made me want to take a step back. "Stop trying to control everything, Devante. This doesn't concern you."

I held up my hand, wishing they would both chill out. "Um, let me get the kids settled." I glanced at the clock on the wall.

"Parents will arrive in about forty minutes, and we'll need some help getting everything downloaded and saved on their flash drives."

I walked away wondering what kind of drama I'd unknowingly invited into the camp.

Tuesday, June 3 at 4:15 p.m.

Kisha was the last child to be picked up. Leesa sent me a text to let me know she was on her way, so Kisha and I waited inside the café. Hailey volunteered to help clean the classroom, but I had a feeling she wanted to linger while Devante packed up his gear. I had never seen her so smitten with a man before.

As Kisha and I made our way toward a booth, we passed Eleanor Olsen sitting in her usual booth. The local mystery author looked up from her laptop and smiled warmly at us.

"How did the photography workshop go today?" Eleanor asked, adjusting her cat-eye reading glasses on her nose.

"It was amazing!" Kisha bounced excitedly. "We learned how to tell stories with a camera."

Eleanor's eyes lit up. "Oh my, that does sound amazing. Stories are my specialty. I'm looking forward to Thursday, when I get to work with you and the other campers."

I touched Kisha's arm. "Miss Eleanor writes mysteries. She's going to teach you some of her writing tips later this week."

"Really? Yesterday, my podcast was about a Squishmallow mystery. We had to write scripts for our podcast."

Eleanor clasped her hands together and chuckled. "I love to hear it. Joss, you have an aspiring mystery writer and podcaster."

Including Eleanor as the final workshop facilitator had been important to me since writing was such a crucial part of media arts. "Maybe Miss Eleanor can help you all create short stories to go with some of your photos from this week."

"That sounds so cool." Kisha turned to me. "Can we sit over there so I can see Mommy when she comes?"

"Good idea." I waved goodbye. "Talk to you later, Eleanor."

We settled a few booths down from Eleanor. While Kisha chatted about today's camp activities, I caught sight of Maya at the café counter placing an order. Ace had a loopy grin on his face, staring at her like a puppy dog. I knew all too well how Maya affected men like that. My brother had been hopelessly in love with her.

"Auntie Joss, I can't wait to show my photos to my mom and dad." Hailey had the idea of attaching the flash drives to colorful lanyards. Despite the bright pink lanyard around her neck, Kisha still gripped the flash drive in her hand like a prized possession. "Today was so fun. I took pictures of everyone."

"Was it better than my class yesterday?" I teased.

Kisha giggled. "No. Not better. I love podcasting too."

I wiped my brow and grinned. "Whew! That's good to hear."

Kisha pointed to the window. "Oh, look. There's Mommy!"

We watched Leesa cross the street. A few seconds later, the café door chimed and she entered.

Kisha jumped up and waved at her mother. "Hey, Mommy! We're over here."

I could tell Leesa had had a day. Her eyes appeared tired, but her grin widened as she approached. "Hey, you! How was camp today?"

Kisha did a little dance, bouncing from one foot to the other. "It was so much fun! We took all kinds of pictures, some with a real camera. Mr. Vante showed us how to make the pictures tell stories. And he's going to give us real pictures we can hold in our hands. Like what's in Grandma Eugeena's photo albums."

"Oh, wow! Sounds like you had another awesome day!"

Leesa sat down across from me, with Kisha squeezing in beside her. "Joss! Girl, I know you must be tired."

Exhaustion had settled into my body, now that I had been sitting still for a few minutes. "Not feeling too bad, but I'm going to sleep good again tonight. Like Kisha said, we had fun!"

"Yes, we did!" Kisha stopped mid-giggle and pointed. "There's our teacher Mr. Vante."

I turned to see Devante crossing through the art center's double doors into the café. Hailey trailed behind him like a groupie. By her hand movements, I could tell she was deep into a conversation. Whether Devante was listening was another matter. From where I sat, he appeared distracted, then his eyes landed on Maya.

Leesa commented. "Wait, I know him. Devante Cavanaugh. I tried to book him as the photographer for our wedding, but we ended up going with Ace instead."

"Small world. How did you hear about him?"

"Instagram." Leesa placed her hands on the table. "I really love the way he captures special emotions with the couples on his feed. Anyway, when I finally got a hold of him, he didn't fit our budget."

"He did today's session for free."

Leesa raised an eyebrow. "Well, that's generous of him. I'm sure it's a good thing for him to show his involvement in the community. I'm happy Kisha and the other kids had fun today." Leesa placed her arms around her daughter's shoulders. "Now we have to get home and figure out dinner. Chris will drop Kisha off in the morning again, and I will see you tomorrow afternoon."

We all scooted out of the booth. "Sounds good," I said. "We need to catch up. It's been a few weeks."

Leesa reached over to hug me. "Girl, it has. Thank you again for pulling this camp together. I wasn't sure what we were going to do when Kisha got out of school."

Kisha clasped her hands together. "Tomorrow, we get to paint. Right, Auntie Joss?"

"That's right. Claude McKnight will be here. Even though we will have some smocks, make sure you don't wear your best clothes."

Leesa nodded. "Thanks for the heads up."

A sharp voice made me jolt in surprise. I spun around toward the voice.

"What have you got against finding out what happened to my brother?" With crossed arms and fiery eyes, Maya glared at Devante.

Devante's wide eyes scanned the café before landing on us. "Maya, please."

There weren't many customers in the café, mostly students studying and Eleanor, who'd stopped tapping on her laptop.

Leesa reached for Kisha, guiding her toward the door. "Looks like you may have some trouble. We're going to go."

I headed over to the counter. Maya was a beautiful woman with an ugly temper that could turn nasty. I'd seen her explode on my brother before. By the time I reached Maya and Devante, my boss appeared, looking perturbed at this disturbance inside her mellow café.

Tre stepped up beside Maya and placed a protective hand on her shoulder. "Hey, keep your cool," he said. But his eyes were fixed on Devante.

Fay looked at Ace first, who stood frozen in place, and then turned her attention to Maya and Devante. "Is everything okay?"

I answered for them, mainly because Maya making a scene annoyed me. Some people loved drama, but I wasn't one of them.

"Maya, I know you had something you wanted to ask me. Maybe we can talk in the center."

Maya rubbed her forehead. "I'm sorry. Yes, please. If we can talk now, that would be great."

We started for the center, and Devante followed. Maya abruptly stopped and held up her hand. "No, you stay out of this."

Tre moved slightly in front of Maya, creating a barrier between her and Devante. "You heard her, man."

Devante faced off with Tre, both men giving each other stony stares. Devante stepped back and pointed toward Maya. "You need to face what happened, both you and Auntie Caroline. Both of you will never heal by stirring up trouble."

Maya glared back. "We need answers."

Tre grabbed her hand. "And we're going to get them."

Maya gazed up at Tre before pushing through the doors ahead of me. Tre shot one last warning look at Devante before following Maya.

Before I could continue behind them, Devante grabbed my arm.

Stunned, I looked down at his hands on my arm and then snatched my arm away. "What are you doing?"

He held up his hands defensively. "I'm sorry. I don't want Maya dragging you into this. I shouldn't have let her talk me into bringing her here today." Devante rubbed his hand over his head. "Thank you for letting me be a part of the camp. I had a lot of fun."

I nodded, still a bit shook. He'd grabbed my arm pretty hard. "I appreciate you spending the day with our campers."

Devante glanced through the double doors before turning to walk away. I hadn't realized Hailey was still there until Devante passed her on the way out the door. With so much going on, I guess she'd hung back for the drama. She walked up to me, her eyes on the door after Devante's exit. "What was that all about? And who was that other guy with Maya?"

"That's Tre Kennedy. He's a spoken word artist. And apparently Maya's boyfriend." I paused. "I'm going to go talk to them. Will you be here tomorrow?"

"Absolutely. I enjoy Claude's work. I plan to be here for the rest of the week, wherever you need me." Hailey pushed her glasses up her nose. "Hey, you be careful. She's kind of scary."

I smiled. "I will. See you tomorrow, Hailey." Taking a breath to brace myself, I pushed the door open. Maya stood in front of one of the local artist exhibits. Tre's arms were wrapped protectively around her shoulders. Unsure where to begin, I walked up beside them and waited.

"I didn't know this was going to be this hard. Why is Devante acting like this?" Maya's voice quavered.

Tre gently rubbed her back. "It's okay, baby. I'm going to wait for you in the car. I'll let you and Joss talk."

Maya hugged Tre. "Thank you for always being here for me."

I watched Tre, waiting until he left, before starting up the conversation. "When you were dating Nate, I never met your brother."

Maya's eyes filled with tears. She quickly swatted them away as if they annoyed her. "My brother went to live with our father when our parents split. He moved back here about seven years ago. We were growing closer, and then he was gone. Our mama's been too broken up to function since he died. She can't get past losing Lens."

Lens.

Then it dawned on me.

Maya McAbee.

Jerome "Lens" McAbee.

"Lens is ...was your brother? I followed him on Instagram. I'm really sorry for your loss. I wish I could've met him. He seemed like such a cool guy."

Maya smiled. "My brother was something special. He got in some trouble when he was younger, but that camera gave him purpose." She blew out a breath. "Look, I know you have had some success with your podcast. I've listened to your first three seasons. I don't know if you plan to do more, but I would love for you to consider taking on Lens's story."

"I thought it was an accidental drowning."

Something flashed in Maya's eyes. "What happened to Lens was no accident. Something was going on with him. He practically told the entire world that in his last IG post."

The one I'd studied last night. I knew it wasn't a coincidence that Maya was coming to me with this proposition. "If you followed my podcast, then you know I have uncovered some pretty scary folks."

"I know. The cops were too quick, insisting Lens accidentally drowned. Someone out there knows what happened."

The weight of Maya's words settled over me like a dark cloud. I agreed. Someone probably knew what happened to Lens. But if Maya was right about her brother being murdered, then whoever killed him was still out there.

Chapter 5
Slice of Truth

Tuesday, June 3 at 6:25 p.m.

I told Maya I would think about what she asked me to do, but I knew where my thoughts leaned. I needed some more time to think about it. Not so much think about it, but to really investigate what happened to Lens leading up to his death, so I could write my questions carefully for the podcast.

I busied myself with making sure the classroom was set up for tomorrow. The painting would be messier than the other sessions, but I felt like we needed to experience the traditional arts too. Each station received a set of prime-colored washable acrylic paints, paintbrushes, a disposable apron, a cup for water and wet wipes for quick cleanups. Satisfied, I closed up the center and returned to the café to see if they needed me.

Fay and Ace were both behind the counter.

"Well?" Fay raised an eyebrow as she wiped down the pastry display case. "You want to tell us what that drama was about?"

Ace, stocking the condiment side bar with sugar packets, turned to face us both. "I can tell you that. Maya wants Joss to investigate Lens's death. Devante, for whatever reason, is opposed to the idea."

I nodded. "He seems to think Maya is stirring up trouble. She thinks there is more to her brother's so-called accidental drowning like you do, Ace. After we talked last night, I looked at Lens's last social media posts. I'm not sure it was a coincidence that Maya showed up here today."

Ace avoided my eyes, concentrating on filling up the creamers. "We talked about trying to get some attention, especially since it's coming up on the anniversary of Lens's death." His shoulders sagged as he peered at me. "I didn't know she was going to come see you."

I shrugged. "I guess she heard about the camp from Devante."

Fay crossed her arms. "Lens's mother Caroline hasn't been as active as she used to be at church. When I saw her a few months ago, it looked like his death has taken a toll on her. I don't know the family dynamics, but maybe Devante wants to protect Caroline."

"That could be true. I wonder if Devante would talk to me."

Ace walked behind the counter. "If he doesn't, I want to be on your podcast. The police didn't bother to talk to me, and Lens and I were close friends. Something was up with him those last few weeks."

Fay looked alarmed. "Ace, honey, if someone really killed that boy, you both could be in danger talking about it openly." She turned to me, her eyes wide behind her glasses. "It's been a while since you've pursued a new season of the podcast."

I nodded. "Six months. But I've had plenty of time off from the *Cold Justice Podcast*. I don't want my listeners to think I've given up on it. Folks are always emailing me or messaging me about cold cases. But I've been more focused on the arts center and getting the summer camp established."

Fay walked back toward her office. "I wondered when you were going to get bitten by inspiration. What do you think your detective boyfriend is going to say about all this?"

I followed her and headed toward the employee lockers outside of her office. "Well, I'm about to find out. That's exactly where I'm heading next. Do you guys want me to help you lock up for the night?"

Fay sat at her desk and picked up the money bag. "No, I think Ace and I have it. You should head out. I know you have to be tired dealing with kids all day."

"It's been fun." I opened my locker and grabbed my purse. "Two more days to go with two of my favorite people. Claude tomorrow and Eleanor on Thursday."

Fay grinned. "You had a great line-up, starting with the famed podcaster yourself. I'm really proud of all that you've accomplished, Joss."

I pulled the strap of my purse over my shoulder, suddenly feeling emotional. "Well, thank you, Fay. That means a lot coming from you."

"You be careful with what you're about to get into."

"I will."

I made my way out front and walked over to where Ace was sweeping the floor. "Hey, I appreciate you volunteering to be a guest. Like Fay said, it may open you up to some unwanted attention. Believe me, I know that from experience."

Ace pulled the broom handle to his chest. "I want to do something. I owe Lens so much for getting me started in photography. I want to keep his legacy going."

"You're doing that in your own way. Your photos are on the wall back there, right next to his."

Ace sighed. "Yeah, but I'm not nearly where he was as an artist."

I touched his shoulder. "You have your own style. And you're still growing. I'll be in touch when I have time to figure out this new season. Are you working tomorrow?"

Ace nodded. "I'll be here."

Navigating the familiar streets away from Sugar Creek's bustling downtown district, passing the mix of historic homes and newer developments that made up our residential neighborhoods, I drove straight to Andre's house. The ten-minute drive gave me time to process everything that had happened today. My mind raced with questions about Lens.

I turned into Andre's neighborhood, admiring the well-maintained craftsman-style homes with their manicured lawns and mature oak trees. Andre's house, a charming two-bedroom bungalow with a cozy front porch, sat on a quiet cul-de-sac. I'd fallen in love with his house the first time I saw it. Sometimes I imagined what it would be like to share a home with Andre.

While I loved living with and getting to know my grandmother, Louise's home wasn't really mine. Andre's place felt like the kind of home where we could build a real life together.

It was the right size for a family. I wondered if we would ever take that next step.

I blew out a breath. I couldn't stand it when I did that. Pondering about the future wasn't always good for my mental health.

What I knew right now, Andre was the one person I wanted to talk to about the case. I didn't need him to talk me out of taking on a new season of the podcast. He knew better than that, but he would at least give me a sense of direction.

Andre's car was in the driveway, but so was a dark SUV I didn't recognize. Andre's partner drove an older Ford Taurus, and I doubted Detective Grayson Beckett had suddenly bought a new vehicle. Andre mentioned being assigned to a task force. Did he invite a colleague to his home?

I should've sent a text before I left the café, but I had assumed Andre would be available. I pulled out my phone, but then my impulses kicked in. My mom had warned me all my life about being impulsive. I hoped I wouldn't regret barging in on my boyfriend and his visitor. I had a key, but I wasn't feeling that bold, so I rang the bell, knowing Andre would see me on his doorbell camera.

Andre opened the door, eyeing me with caution. Probably because I was giving him the *Who do you have in here?* look.

He beckoned me inside. "Hey! Come on in."

Feeling silly, I stepped past him into the living room. Then I caught sight of Andre's visitor. Before I could stop myself, I blurted. "What are you doing here?"

Tuesday, June 3 at 7:11 p.m.

Looking entirely too comfortable, Nate leaned back in the chair near the couch and gave me a half-hearted wave. "What's up, little sis?"

After getting over my initial shock, my face grew warm with anger. I crossed my arms and looked back and forth from Andre to Nate. This was highly suspicious. Sure, Andre was a likable guy, but my brother barely spoke to me and I had no idea why. Two days in a row, these two were looking like partners in crime.

"What is going on? Why are you two hanging out with each other?"

"Joss—" Andre started.

The smirk on Nate's face deepened, showing off his dimples. "What's your problem? I thought you'd be happy that I like him. Most of your past boyfriends haven't been worth two cents."

Offended, I placed my hands on my hips. "How do you know that? You haven't even been around."

Nate leaned forward and shook his head. "Don't need to. Mama tells me everything."

"What?" That was the last thing I needed to hear. I shacked up for a year with my previous boyfriend before moving in with my grandmother. My mother had plenty of choice words during that period of my life. I knew nothing about Nate's life, but apparently my mother told him all my business.

Andre stepped up behind me and started rubbing my shoulder. "Okay, you two. Joss, why don't you sit down? I know you have to be tired from running the camp all day. You hungry?"

"Yeah." I mumbled as I went over to the couch and sank down onto it.

"We got pizza. I didn't know if you were stopping by, but I have your favorite with mushrooms and bell peppers."

That put a smile on my face. Andre didn't even know if I was coming over, but he'd ordered my favorite pizza toppings for me.

My brother scrunched up his face. "Ew! That's no way to eat a pizza. At least you're finally out of that pineapple stage."

I scooted to the edge of the couch. "I still enjoy pineapples on my pizza too, not that it's any of your concern." I may have missed my older brother, but I didn't miss him picking on me.

"Can we try to get along?" Andre joked as he set a paper plate with two slices of pizza along with a can of Pepsi in front of me. He sat down on the other side of the couch in between me and Nate.

I picked up my pizza slice and took a bite, savoring the familiar combination of mushrooms and bell peppers. But the comfort food wasn't shaking the weird feeling I had about finding my brother and boyfriend hanging out together.

"So, tell us about your day." Andre settled back into the couch.

I chewed thoughtfully, still eyeing the two of them. "My day was... interesting." I set down my plate and gave Nate my own smirk. I might not have seen my brother that much the past few years, but we slipped right back into old habits like it was yesterday. "You'll never guess who showed up at camp."

Nate raised an eyebrow. "Who?"

"Maya."

My brother's eyes widened and his face softened into that puppy dog look. He tentatively said her name as if he couldn't process what I said. "Ma...Maya?"

"Yep. Your ex-girlfriend walked through the door this morning as Devante Cavanaugh's assistant."

Nate's reaction shifted as he narrowed his eyes, sitting up straighter in the seat. "So she came to help with the camp?"

"I know, right? I couldn't believe it. Not perfect Maya. But I soon found out she had an agenda."

Watching the exchange between us, Andre leaned in with a worried look on his face. "What kind of agenda?"

"She wants me to talk about her brother's death on the podcast. I don't know if you know about him. Jerome McAbee a.k.a. "Lens." He was a popular local photographer with a huge social media presence. He supposedly drowned near the port about two years ago. A lot of people think he had some help getting in that water."

Nate glanced at Andre. "You really let her pursue these cases?"

"Let me! This is my podcast, and I choose the cases. And how do you keep in touch with your ex-girlfriend and not your own family?"

Andre and Nate exchanged a look again that made my stomach clench.

"Okay, that's it." I pointed my finger from one to the other. "What's going on here? The way you're both acting tells me there's something I don't know."

Andre cleared his throat. "Joss. Please."

"No. I'm tired of being left out of conversations." I crossed my arms and glared at my brother. I felt like some snotty teen having a crash out, but my instincts were on alert. "Nate, why are you really back here?"

The silence turned awkward until Andre finally spoke. "Nate, tell her."

"Tell me what?"

My brother rubbed his forehead, a gesture I remembered from childhood when he was about to confess to something. "Joss, there are things about my life... about what I do for work... that I haven't told you."

My shoulders tensed even more. "What kinds of things?"

Nate's face grew hard in a way I'd never seen. "The kind that could get people hurt if the wrong people found out. Including you and Mom."

A chill ran down my spine. This time, my voice came out low and shaky. "Nate. What do you do for a living?"

He looked at Andre again, who nodded encouragingly. "I'm a federal agent, Joss. DEA. Have been for almost three years now."

I stared at him, then back at Andre, certain I'd misheard. "You're what?"

Tuesday, June 3 at 7:01 p.m.

I'm not sure how long it took me to register what my brother told me, but when it clicked, I jumped up. "How are you in law enforcement and I didn't know this? Mom doesn't know this either?"

Nate threw his hands in the air. "See! This is why I didn't want to say anything."

Andre gently wrapped his hands around my arm and guided me back to the couch. "Give your brother a chance to explain."

"Explain. He knows I work at a café and that I produce a podcast. And Mom has probably been telling him all of my business. Yet, I don't know what he does for a living. I don't even know where he lives."

Nate let out a long sigh. "I didn't want to worry both of you."

That had me standing up again. "Dude, we worried about you anyway. You've communicated so sporadically."

"It would have been different if you knew," he protested.

"Really? Do you think we're weak females who couldn't handle it? Guess what? Oh, wait. You already know. I'm dating a detective."

I started pacing in front of the coffee table. "I can't wait until Mom finds out. She's going to rip you—"

Nate stood, towering over me. "You can't tell her."

"What?" I placed my hands on my hips, looking up at him as if he was some alien. He might as well be. I didn't know this man even if he did resemble our dad and had our mother's eyes.

Behind me, I heard Andre say, "Man, that's crazy. You need to come clean. This is no time for you to keep this to yourself."

I spun around and looked at Andre. "Right! Please talk some sense into him."

Nate sat back down. "I can't do this right now."

Andre stood and reached for me. "Joss, sit back down. I know you're upset, but hear your brother out. This is important."

I wasn't sure if I could sit down. Nate left Charleston shortly after Dad died. It was bad enough losing our dad, then my brother left. Because I had a reasonable boyfriend, I sat back down next to him.

I took some deep breaths. Then I focused on my uneaten pizza on the coffee table. I grabbed the plate and started chewing. Perfect time for comfort food. In between bites, I asked, "So you're a DEA agent? What's DEA stand for, anyway? I've heard it before."

Nate nodded, "Drug Enforcement Agency."

I frowned. "How did you get started?"

Nate answered, "When I left here after Dad died, I enlisted in the Army."

I choked out, "Army? You were in the Army and we didn't even know?" My brother really lived this whole life away from here, away from us.

Nate raised an eyebrow. "Yeah. When I decided not to re-enlist, my captain encouraged me to check out the DEA, said it was a good job to take on for guys with military experience. I've been in about three years now."

My head was spinning. "I still don't understand why you didn't tell us. It's not like you're a spy in the CIA."

Nate wouldn't look at me. "I told Dad. I mean it was one of the last conversations we had. He wanted me to finish school, take up business or accounting like him and Mom. I knew I needed something more physical to do than sit in an office." He crossed his arms. "I told Dad I was thinking about joining the Army or the Marines. Being an athlete, he got where I was coming from and told me to go for it. He warned me Mom wouldn't be happy."

"You could've at least told me!" I shouted. "And what does Mom think you do for a living?"

Nate sighed and rubbed his head. "Security consulting."

I rolled my eyes. "That's pretty vague." I turned to Andre, who'd been quietly listening back and forth. "How did you find him?"

Andre grinned. "I'm a detective, remember."

I stuffed the pizza crust in my mouth to keep from saying anything else.

Andre continued, "You were really worried about your brother, so I wondered about his job. In law enforcement, there is always somebody who knows somebody. I asked Detective Amos Jones and he helped me out."

I tilted my head. "Really?" Amos Jones was a retired detective who lived next door to my grandmother with his wife, Eugeena.

Andre looked at Nate. "Yeah, Detective Jones knew your DEA Special Agent in Charge from back in the day, said they were rookies together. Even with the contact info, I wasn't sure I could reach you."

I tossed my empty plate on the coffee table and looked at Andre. "You still had trouble reaching him?"

Andre peered at Nate. "Are you ready?"

Nate licked his lips. "Not really, but I've come this far." My brother looked at me. "I've been working undercover for a year and a half in Atlanta. My cover might have gotten blown a few weeks ago, so I'm back home for now."

I had no words. I stared at this man who I'd grown up with, trying to process who'd he become. When I could finally string some words together, I asked, "Are you in danger?"

What I really wanted to ask.

Did you bring danger with you?

Chapter 6

Percolating Pressure

Wednesday, June 4 at 8:30 a.m.

I didn't sleep well last night despite being exhausted. My brother's latest bombshell, that he'd been working undercover, left me contemplating what it meant for him now. I watched plenty of cop shows and knew the risks of going undercover from a fictional show. If my brother's cover was blown, what did that mean for his future? All this time, I'd been upset by my brother's absence.

And he'd been risking his life.

Though I didn't have the complete details of the operation, I got the gist that something went wrong, and Nate needed to leave Atlanta. But for how long? Nate couldn't answer that question.

Andre and I both agreed he couldn't keep this from our mother. Since Nate was staying at the house, there were bound to be opportunities to talk to her. This was one time I didn't wish to be a fly on the wall. Clarice Miller had a quiet demeanor until you made her angry.

Once I arrived at the center, I did my best to focus on what would probably be our messiest workshop. Hailey arrived earlier than she did yesterday. After a cup of coffee and one of Fay's decadent sweet potato muffins, we went to work covering the tables with white plastic tablecloths.

"These are so cute," Hailey commented as we set up wood easels on each desk.

"Aren't they? Claude and I found them a few weeks ago at that new craft shop."

Hailey's eyes widened behind her glasses. "Oooh, I haven't been there yet. Hard to believe that just two years ago this place used to be a craft shop."

It was hard to believe. Especially since the owner died not too long after giving me a few choice words about my first season of the *Cold Justice Podcast*. After my second podcast season, things got real when I unknowingly provoked Rebecca Montgomery's killer to come after me. Though I still had some mental scars, thankfully, Rebecca's killer was behind bars.

With help from some local funders like the tech company, Synaptic, we converted the empty craft shop into the Rebecca

Montgomery Art Center. We'd been using the center for the café's popular Friday Night Jam twice a month, local authors' book signings, and Fay rotated a gallery exhibit featuring local artists.

This summer's arts camp was the first of many educational opportunities. Despite the drama yesterday, the camp was going well.

The morning went by pretty quickly. Claude McKnight moved between the tables with the patience of a seasoned teacher, offering gentle guidance and encouragement. "Remember, there's no wrong way to paint your favorite place," Claude said, pausing beside Amani's canvas. "Art is about how you see the world, not how others think you should see it."

Amani beamed as she added another stroke of purple to her interpretation of Rainbow Row. "I made the houses different colors than they really are because that's how I would paint them."

"That's perfect," Claude smiled. "I love the bold colors."

I watched from the back of the room, happy to see Claude connecting with the kids. Rebecca had been his friend and a painter as well, so I knew this had to be special to him being able to carry on her legacy.

Hailey and I set up a drying area where we could hang the finished paintings. The afternoon sun streaming through the large windows would help speed the process.

"These turned out beautifully," Hailey said, carefully hanging Amani's "Rainbow Row."

I secured Kisha's painting of the inside of the South Carolina Aquarium to the makeshift clothesline we'd strung across one corner of the room. Kisha had drawn one of the big tanks and filled it with colorful fish. "They're all natural artists."

Hailey asked, "I don't know how you stay so busy. I heard you're starting up another season of the podcast."

I froze. "Oh, did I mention that to you yesterday?"

Hailey's eyes widened behind her glasses. "No. I saw it on social media, which surprised me. You hadn't said anything, and I know how excited you get about starting a new season."

I hadn't even decided if I was going to do the season yet.

What is going on?

Wednesday, June 4 at 2:00 p.m.

Was I ready to start a new podcast season? Lens's story fit perfectly, but I needed more information to plan a full season. Right now, all I had was Maya and Ace for potential guests. I didn't know who else to talk to about Lens. And the most important part of the research hadn't taken place. I still needed to talk to my inside man. My goal last night was to talk it through with Andre, but my plans were sidetracked thanks to my brother and his bombshell confessions.

"Where did you see this announcement?"

"Hold on. Maybe it was an older post." Her glasses slid down her nose as she pulled out her phone. Her brows furrowed in concentration over her frames. "I need to find where I saw it. I was looking at Devante's profile last night... to, um, see if he posted anything about the camp."

I raised an eyebrow. Homegirl was stalking the man. "Did he post anything?"

Hailey wrinkled her nose. "No, he didn't. But you know how Instagram will show you other people to follow. I recognized the woman who came to help yesterday. I forgot her name, but I clicked on her profile. Wait, here she is." She handed me her phone.

I studied the screen and saw the reel with Maya talking. "Can you turn the volume on?"

"Sure," Hailey leaned down and clicked the sound icon on the video.

@MayaMacStyle: Hey fam! This isn't my usual content, but I had to share with you all that someone is going to tell my brother's story. Thank you @JossMiller for agreeing to investigate what really happened to Romeo Lens on the *Cold Justice Podcast*. Stay tuned for the first episode when it drops. #ColdJustice #RomeoLens

My stomach dropped.

No, she didn't!

The post already had hundreds of likes and comments. Talking more to myself, I mumbled, "I hadn't confirmed I was doing this yet."

Hailey stared at me. "Are you serious? Oh no, Joss. What are you going to do?"

I shook my head. "I don't have a choice now. I'm mean, I told her I would think about it, but I wanted to get past the camp. And Friday Night Jam is this week. Plus, these episodes take time to research."

I placed my hands together over my head as if that would slow down the mounting frustration. Then I closed my eyes and breathed.

Oh, Lord! Help me!

Hailey touched my arm, her voice so low I could barely hear her. "Joss, are you okay? Maybe we should go inside the café. You know, take a break."

My eyes shot open. "No. Let's get back to the kids. *This* can wait until later."

We spent the next hour helping the kids hang up their paintings to dry as they finished them. Since we had a lot more supplies today, I assigned each kid chores to help us clean up the classroom faster. By the time the first parent arrived, we had the classroom back to normal.

Claude came over while I finished stuffing the last of the disposable tablecloths into a trash bag. "Hey, Joss, you need some help?"

"Sure, can you help me take this trash to the dumpster?"

Claude grabbed three bags while I got the last one. "Lead the way."

Grateful for the help, I headed down the hallway toward the back door that led to the dumpsters. I unlocked the deadbolt on the door. For a split second, the sunshine felt good on my face. Then I caught a whiff of the dumpster and wrinkled my nose. The closer we drew to the dumpster, the more I realized how humid it had gotten. That wasn't helping matters either.

There used to be a fence that separated the café's dumpster, but since we connected the center to the café, it was now a wide open space of concrete with both dumpsters side-by-side. Apparently, the waste management folks hadn't come yet. The café dumpster was overflowing.

Claude heaved the trash bags over into the center's dumpster and then helped me with mine. We both wasted no time scrambling back inside. I locked the back door, then checked it for good measure. I'd had an issue with a back door once that I never wanted repeated.

As we passed the classroom, Claude asked, "Do you need help with anything else?"

I shook my head. "No, I think we're good. I really appreciate you sharing your time with us. This was a bit of an experiment, and I'm really glad you took part. We'll wrap up the camp tomorrow with Eleanor's writing workshop."

"I know she will love that. Thanks for including me in the camp, Joss. This was a lot of fun. At first I wasn't sure about it; I spend so much time alone painting. But this was good. You have some talented kids."

"You're good with kids!" I reached up and hugged him. "I hope I can call on you again."

"Absolutely." Claude stepped back and tilted his head to the side. "Is everything okay? I couldn't help but notice you seemed frustrated earlier when you were talking to Hailey. It didn't have to do with the camp or anything?"

I blew out a breath. "No, camp has been great. I got pushed into something that I wanted to think about some more." I explained to Claude about the *pending* podcast season highlighting Romeo Lens.

"Wow, that's awful. This Maya person seems pretty desperate. But for the headache that it's caused you, it sounds like Lens's death needs further investigation." Claude rubbed his chin. "I didn't know him personally, but I remember Lens's dad."

"Really? How did you know him?"

Claude crossed his arms. "Well, my father knew him. They grew up together. In fact, there are some of his paintings at the house."

"Oh, so art ran in the family. What was his name?"

"Lance McAbee. I can send you some photos of the paintings my dad has. I still haven't dismantled my dad's office. It's the same as it was before he died."

Sounded like my dad's office, and my dad had been gone almost eight years. My mother had given away his clothes and other items, but she kept his office the same.

"Thanks, Claude. I would love to see them. I know Lens lived with his father, so I imagine his dad was a great influence on his photography."

"I bet! Well, I'm going to head into the café to speak to Fay. I'll tune in when your new season starts. And, Joss. Don't worry about this, you're a pro at producing podcasts now. You got this!"

I smiled. "I appreciate your encouragement."

Now that I was alone, the frustration from earlier crept back in. My first thought was to go vent to Fay, but I already knew what my boss and surrogate big sister would tell me

Handle your business, girl!

So, I went to the center's office and pushed the door closed before pulling out my phone. I would handle this by sending Maya a direct message.

@JossMiller: I saw your Instagram post. I was planning to do the podcast, but that wasn't right to announce it before I confirmed with you. I still need time to prepare, so I will be in touch.

The response came back almost immediately.

@MayaMacStyle: I'm SO sorry! I thought you had decided last night. I'll delete the post if you want, but so many people responded. I was wrong to jump ahead like that. Can we record this weekend? I feel like I should be in the first episode, but I need to go out of town next week.

I stared at the message for a full minute. Finally, I closed my mouth and bowed my head, doing the only thing I knew to do.

"Lord, I know Maya is grieving her brother, but I don't want to be pushed into this either. If it's in your will, I will move forward with this platform you blessed me with. I pray that Maya and her family receive some closure."

I never considered my podcast to be a source for finding answers. When I started the first season, my goal was to pay tribute to my murdered grandfather, a man I'd never known. I wanted people to know what happened to him and remember the legacy he left with his short life.

The same was true for Rebecca Montgomery during the second season. A talented artist whose life was snuffed out far too soon. She'd left beautiful, thought-provoking murals all over the community. I wanted people to know the person behind those murals. I had no idea her killer would be exposed. Or that he would come after me.

The podcast had grown into something beyond what I could ever have conceived. Somehow, dots got connected as people talked and shared their points of view with me. I was thankful God allowed my little podcast to be the vehicle for justice.

Feeling less stressed, I focused on the screen and started typing.

@JossMiller: Don't delete the post. But next time, check with me first. We can meet on Saturday.

@MayaMacStyle: Thank you!! I appreciate you so much.

I didn't think it was a good idea for Maya to thank me yet.

Chapter 7

In A Jam

Thursday, June 5 at 5:10 p.m.

I'd made a mistake. Fay warned me, but like my mother often said, I could be hard-headed sometimes. This was one of those occasions. Eleanor did a great job today, closing out the last day of camp. In fact, we talked about her doing a full week of camp in the future.

After swinging her bag over her shoulders, Eleanor's eyes twinkled. "We can use the entire camp for the campers to brainstorm, write their stories, draw illustrations and layout their design. There are companies we can ship the books to to make real books."

"I love that idea, Eleanor. The kids enjoyed you today. Let's talk about it some more."

With less cleanup today, I closed up and dropped into the café. There was no sign of Ace today, but there were two new baristas at the counter. Summer brought more tourists to town and to the café. There were always college students spending their summer making money at Sugar Creek Café. They came and went every year, like Hailey, who now worked as an elementary teacher.

Fay took one look at me. "Are you sure you're going to be able to handle tomorrow night?"

I grimaced. "It will be fine." Said the person who felt like she'd aged ten years in four days. I'd had a lot of fun, but I had also spent more time around kids this week than ever. I admired teachers who spent ten months of the year with tons of students.

Fay thought I was being overly ambitious having the camp the same week as our Friday Night Jam. The community loved Friday Night Jam, and it gave more exposure to the art center.

As Fay's assistant manager, my role had evolved beyond being a barista to social media manager and event planner. But I didn't mind. I had a knack for it.

I crossed over to the locker and pulled out my bag. "After resting up tonight and tomorrow, I should be good."

Fay peeked at me over her burgundy glasses. My boss changed eyeglass frames every week; she had so many pairs. "If you say so.

I heard you're starting a new podcast season. Can I still count on you to help here at the café?"

I opened my mouth in shock. "Of course. You know most of my recording and editing time happens on the weekend or in the evenings."

My boss threw her head back and laughed. "I was joking, Joss. You know I want you to take the role of managing the art center more seriously. You're already doing the work. And it's summer, I have plenty of baristas right now."

"I noticed the two new ones out front, but I love this place." The arts center was so big, sometimes it felt like an empty museum. This week had been great with the kids in there all day and parents and caregivers stopping by. I also loved it when people were in there for Friday Night Jam, but I loved the vibe of greeting customers and getting their orders. I wasn't ready to give that up.

My phone buzzed. I looked down to see Andre's name appear on the screen. "This is my man. Let me see what's up."

Fay cackled as I walked toward the kitchen sink area.

"Hey," I answered.

"How did the last day of camp go?" Andre's voice sounded tired like mine.

"Good. Eleanor's writing workshop was a hit." I rubbed my temples. "Now I need to rest up for Friday Night Jam tomorrow."

"Speaking of Friday Night Jam..." Andre paused, and I could hear the reluctance in his voice. "I'm not going to be able to help with setup tomorrow night. This task force thing is about to take over my life this weekend."

My heart sank. The entire weekend! Andre always helped me set up, moving chairs and even checking people in at the door. And we hadn't spent any time together this week. At least alone time.

"They're making you work the whole weekend?"

"We're following up on some leads that can't wait." His voice softened. "I'm sorry, babe. I'm going to miss you."

"I'll miss you too, but I understand." I didn't really, but I wasn't about to make my boyfriend feel bad.

"We haven't talked, but it sounds like you're going through with the podcast on Lens." Andre was quiet for a moment. "Joss, I need you to be careful. I know I always say that with all the podcast seasons, but I mean it. Keep me updated."

Panic gurgled in my stomach. I placed my hand over my belly. "Is there something you know that you can't tell me?"

"I did some asking around about Lens. Of course Detective Wilkes found out."

"Oops. I hope I didn't get you in trouble."

Andre laughed softly. "She's familiar with your podcast and my relationship with you. In fact, she's the one who dropped this warning. Wilkes heard Lens might have been caught up in something illegal before he died."

Remembering I was still in the café's kitchen, I caught myself before I spoke too loud. Fay's office wasn't that far away; she'd probably already heard my one-sided conversation. "Caught up in something, or caught someone else doing something?"

Another pause. "I can't give you specifics. But if Lens was investigating something dangerous, or if he was involved in something he shouldn't have been, you need to be careful. I'm curious about who you're going to get to talk on the podcast."

"Me too. I only have two people so far. That's not much of a season."

"Well, if anything feels off, call me. Day or night, task force or no task force."

"I will." I fretted with my bag, feeling worried. "Andre?"

"Yeah?"

"Be careful yourself, okay? Whatever this task force is working on."

"I will. Love you, Joss."

"Love you too."

Our conversation continued to echo in my mind as I said goodnight to Fay and during my drive home.

Caught up in something, or caught someone else?

I didn't know Lens, but it felt more logical that the artist caught something. Why else did they never recover his missing camera equipment?

Friday, June 6 at 6:00 p.m.

When I arrived at the café, I felt energized for tonight's Friday Night Jam. I waved to Ace and the two newest baristas, who were all behind the counter, taking care of customers. The café stayed open a few hours longer than usual, allowing guests to go back and forth. I put my bag in the locker and grabbed the programs I'd picked up from our local printer down the street. Before I headed back up front, I surveyed the rows of cupcakes Fay had made especially for tonight. The jam was a lot of work, but it was good for business.

I pushed open the double doors and found a buzz of activity inside the center. Despite no Andre tonight, the burgundy cushioned chairs had already been arranged to face the small performance area on the back wall. Fay's boyfriend, Joe Phillips, was adjusting the height on a microphone stand while Fay observed.

"Wow, you guys started setting up early."

Fay grinned. "We figured you could use the help. It's been a busy week for you. Looking at your lineup for tonight, we're probably going to have a good crowd. Some regulars, plus a few tourists."

"I'm excited about the crowd and I appreciate y'all jumping in to help. I'm going to set up by the door."

Since we had a little more of a budget, I'd invested in a fancy whiteboard and corkboard combination on wheels for signage by the door. Tonight, I'd added photos of the entertainment to the board. Inside the programs were writeups about each artist and a handy coupon that could be redeemed for a cup of coffee from Sugar Creek Café.

Singer Lily Hartman would open the jam tonight. My last podcast season was about Lily's deceased husband, choir director Victor Hartman. Since the outcome of that podcast had brought some closure, the young widow had become a jam participant I could always count on. It was good seeing her sing again after taking a break.

After Lily, there would be two spoken word artists. One of them, Anita Stewart, was new to Friday Night Jam. We didn't have a DJ tonight; Nyla B. Masters was out of town for a gig. She'd suggested Anita to me, and I liked what she'd posted on social media.

Tre Kennedy, a spoken word artist who liked to go by Da-TruthPoetry online, was not new to Friday Night Jam. I'd spent most of the day researching Lens online, diving deep into his Instagram followers. The detective work gave me ideas for other guests. Lens had been part of a tight-knit circle of Charleston artists and activists. Several familiar faces appeared in his photos. One of them was Tre, and I hoped he would be open to the idea of being on the podcast, especially since it appeared he had a relationship with Maya.

I was really excited about the local comedian rounding out tonight's talent, Malik Porter. I always stopped to watch his gut-busting reels on Instagram. To my surprise, he lived right here in Charleston.

Even though we had great sponsorship for the arts center, we charged a small cover charge to provide an honorarium to the entertainers. I placed the small cash box and a roll of tickets by the door. Door prizes were a must! Our main sponsor Synaptic had donated some cool noise canceling headphones. Different store owners on the block also donated books and hoodies, and there were Sugar Creek Café mugs.

I settled onto a stool by the entrance and soon fell into a rhythm of collecting money and tearing off perforated tickets. As usual, we had a pretty diverse crowd, from college students to couples, and several groups of women.

Grateful for a lull in traffic, I grabbed a swig of water. It was a good thing I swallowed before I looked up to catch who'd entered the center.

I was pretty sure I would have choked.

Friday, June 6 at 6:45 p.m.

Maya sauntered through the door followed by a petite woman with a honey blond pixie cut. She was a pretty woman with her face as heavily made up as Maya's. What had my attention more was my brother standing behind the women.

"Joss, I love that you have these events in Sugar Creek for the arts." Maya glanced back as though she didn't know my brother was behind her. Placing her hands on her mouth, she batted her eyes. "Would you look at this sibling love? You even have your brother coming out. The Nate I knew only did sporting events and action movies."

I gave Nate a side eye, wondering what was up. I took it from the frown on his face he hadn't expected Maya.

"At least you know me here. This man tried to ignore me when I saw him in Atlanta a few weeks ago." Maya shook her head as if disgusted then dug into her small gold purse. She pulled out a ten-dollar bill. "Two tickets, please. Like really, I thought we broke up on good terms. He didn't have to ignore me like that. It was so embarrassing."

Before I could pass her the tickets, she pulled out her phone.

"Joss, would you mind if I get a picture with you? I'd love to share it on my IG."

I felt my smile falter, but Maya didn't give me a chance to object. She rushed to my side and shoved the camera phone in front of us.

This woman has boundary issues.

I attempted to smile, but I was sure it probably looked like a grimace instead. Usually I would have put more effort into my appearance, but it had been a long week. I'd managed to pull my hair up into a puff, add my favorite gold hoops and some lip gloss. Maya's face was beat perfectly with makeup, and her silky black hair poured down her shoulders. I did like the off the shoulder gold top she was wearing. I gave her props for that.

The woman who came with her stepped forward. "I'm Zara, by the way. Zara Cavanaugh." She had a slight accent I couldn't place, and her handshake was firm. "Maya told me you're looking into Lens's case for the podcast."

My attention sharpened. Another person connected to Lens? And her last name was Cavanaugh. Possibly Devante's sister.

"You knew Lens?"

Zara's hazel eyes grew sad. "We dated before he died. I was probably the last person to see him alive that night."

Dated? Last person to see him alive!

I tried to make sense in my head knowing Devante, Maya, and Lens were related. "Maybe we can talk more?"

"She would love that," Maya interjected. "You need to hear what she has to say. Put her down for an episode."

"What?" Zara's eyes widened. "Maya, I'm not sure that's a good idea."

"Don't worry, Joss will take care of you." She stabbed a pointy, gold bedazzled fingernail in my direction. "You're going to give me the time we're meeting tomorrow, right?"

I nodded. "Early afternoon? It will be an online recording, so I'll send the link to your email tonight or in the morning."

"That's perfect," Maya said. She grabbed Zara's hand. "Let's grab some seats."

Maya and Zara found seats toward the front. Instead of sitting down, Maya whipped out her phone and started recording herself with her back to the stage.

"Hey, Sis." Nate stood in front of the table where I sat and passed me a five-dollar bill. "Looks like a good crowd."

I turned my focus to my brother. "Definitely. For a second there, I thought you came with Maya."

He rolled his eyes. "Not a chance. Look, I know I was smitten with her for years, but I've traveled around the world a bit since her."

"I'm glad to hear you've gotten over her. Good for you ignoring her in Atlanta. She acts like the world revolves around her." I studied his face. "Hopefully, there isn't someone else you're keeping from me and Mom."

Nate rubbed his hands across his freshly trimmed goatee. "Not at the moment. I'm going to grab some of this performance. I knew Lily back in the day. It will be good to hear her sing."

I watched my brother sit on the other side toward the middle. I laughed to myself at how far away he made sure he sat from his ex-girlfriend. I remembered Maya being high maintenance when she dated my brother, she seemed even more so now. I guess that came with living your life in the spotlight on social media.

Tre Kennedy came from the back where we had set up a classroom as a makeshift green room. Maya must have caught sight of him, I heard her squeal. The crowd quieted and turned as Maya ran up to Tre and hugged him.

With my eyes on Maya and Tre, I didn't notice that Ace had come up behind me. "Hey, Joss."

I held my hands to my chest from the slight scare. First, there was Maya's squealing and now, Ace sneaking up on me.

Ace peered in the direction where I'd been looking. "We have a lot of folks tonight. How did we do?"

I patted the cash box. "Not bad. Fay will be pleased."

Ace leaned forward, narrowing his eyes. "Is that Maya with Tre Kennedy?"

"Yeah, she came in with a woman. Zara Cavanaugh. She said she dated Lens."

Ace's face grew hard. "She's here too!" He paused and then grabbed a seat to pull it up next to me. "She was Lens's girlfriend. But she's with Devante now. They got married earlier this year."

"Wait, what?" I felt my eyebrows shoot up. Devante's profile was filled with wedding portraits, but I hadn't realized he was a recent newlywed. "He married his cousin's girl."

Ace shook his head as if he still couldn't believe it. "Crazy, right? They started being together maybe six months after Lens died. Some people thought it was weird, her moving on with a relative so fast."

I commented. "Grief affects people differently, I guess."

Ace smirked. "Or they were together before Lens died."

That could be a possibility too.

"Welcome to Friday Night Jam at Sugar Creek Café," Fay announced from the microphone. "Tonight, we have a fantastic lineup of local talent. First up, let's welcome my friend Lily Hartman!"

If I had any doubts about investigating Lens's death for this podcast season, they all disappeared. The relationship dynamics of Lens's family had me intrigued.

Friday, June 6 at 7:29 p.m.

After Lily's set ended and applause died down, Fay returned to the microphone. "Thank you, Lily! Next up, we have another Friday Night Jam favorite, spoken word artist Tre Kennedy!"

While Lily belted out tunes, I'd closed up my makeshift ticket area and took the cashbox to Fay's office. On the way back, I grabbed a chair by my brother. It wasn't until Tre stood up that I noticed he'd been sitting next to Maya. I side-eyed my brother, who I felt stiffen beside me. I wondered if Nate was really over his ex-girlfriend.

Tre strode up to the small stage area. He gripped the microphone stand. "Good evening, Sugar Creek, I'm Tre Kennedy. I'm not from around here originally, but Charleston has a way of calling people back, doesn't it? You can miss the history of this place. You can feel it in the air."

Next to me, Nate went still. I glanced over and caught him studying Tre, his jaw set as if he was angry. When he noticed me looking, he relaxed his face, but kept his eyes on the stage.

Was my brother jealous of Maya's man?

Though I'd seen him many times before, I tried to examine Tre from a different viewpoint. I wouldn't really call Tre handsome; he had a sculpted face with high cheekbones framed by a well-groomed goatee and a low fade haircut. With the lights we had installed around the stage, his chocolate skin glistened and his eyes sparkled as he gazed over the crowd. This was all a part of Tre's act to mesmerize the crowd before he assaulted them with his wordplay for the evening. I'd seen him do this countless times. Tonight, he didn't seem to have the same easy smile. I wondered what words he would gift us.

When he spoke, his deep voice wavered a bit as if he felt a heavy weight. "Tonight, I want to dedicate my set to someone who understood that call to Charleston better than most. A friend we lost too soon. Some of y'all knew him as simply Lens."

From the corner of my eye, I saw a movement. Maya stood with her camera recording. Tre smiled and winked at her like some movie star. Then bowed his head for a moment as if in prayer. He lifted his head and gazed directly into the crowd.

Behind the lens, he walked these streets.
Not as a collector of things, but of truth.
Each click of the shutter, small rebellion against forgetting.
Some folks didn't like what he chose to remember.
Preferring those stories stayed buried.
But he knew the lens reveals what the heart refuses to see
That painful truths can't stay hidden forever.
We who remain must be the lens now.
We must focus on what matters.

The applause came quick, and some stood on their feet as Tre bowed his head. He stepped off the stage toward Maya, who reached up and hugged him.

Once again, I looked at my brother. I couldn't read his face as he watched Maya and Tre embrace, but something had shifted in his posture. His jaw was tight. Suddenly he stood. "I'll catch you later, Sis."

Just like that, my brother was gone.

Maybe he still had feelings for Maya.

I turned back to the couple, wanting to know more about Tre's words.

Some folks didn't like what he chose to remember.

What folks? Did Tre know something?

Chapter 8

Muddy Waters

Saturday, June 7 at 1:10 p.m.

She was late!

I'd woken up around eight o'clock Saturday morning to make sure I set up the remote interview inside Zoom with Maya. She'd responded to my email and text that she'd received the one o'clock invite. I'd gone over my questions for Maya twice, set up my microphone, noise-canceling headphones and a ring light that made me look more awake than I felt.

I scrolled through the *Cold Justice Podcast* analytics while I waited, trying to quiet the anxiety churning in my stomach. Season one about my grandfather's murder had reached 250,000 downloads. Season two, Rebecca Montgomery's disappearance, hit 300,000 downloads. Season three had become my best season, coming in at almost a million downloads. It thrilled me, my little podcast had snagged attention within the wide pool of true crime podcasts available.

A comment from a listener caught my eye.

"Joss gives voices to the voiceless. She doesn't stop until the truth comes out."

Another read, *"This podcast changed how I see cold cases. Real people, real pain, real justice."*

Real danger too, I thought, thinking about the attack during my second season. I didn't take it for granted when Andre, Fay, and my mom warned me to be careful. I still had the occasional nightmare about my ordeal.

The longer Maya took to show up, the more I wondered if maybe she'd changed her mind. There was no doubt Maya enjoyed the spotlight. She'd provided great coverage of Friday Night Jam on her social media. I could have done without her taking a photo of me. I did indeed look as I'd imagined. My eyes were too wide and my smile looked contrived in my haste to look good after having a phone camera shoved in my face.

A notification popped up.

Maya McAbee has entered the waiting room.

"It's about time!" As soon as I clicked the "Admit" button, Maya's face filled my MacBook screen. Behind her was a bookshelf adorned with books, candles, African American figurines, and framed photos. I recognized the setup often displayed in her Instagram reels.

"Hi, Joss," Maya said breathlessly. "I'm so sorry that I'm late. I told my mama what I was doing, and she had a meltdown."

"Oh no. Do you still want to do this?"

Maya arched an eyebrow. "Of course. We need to get the word out. Somebody knows what really happened to my brother."

"Okay. I sent you the questions this morning via email. Sometimes during the conversation, I may come up with other questions."

Maya nodded, squaring her shoulders. "It's fine. Do I look okay?"

"No one will see this video. I only use the audio for the podcast."

"Oh." Maya looked disappointed. "Okay."

"Before we get started with the interview," I said, "I wanted to ask you about Tre Kennedy. His performance last night was really moving. Did you know he was going to dedicate his set to Lens?"

Maya's face lit up. "Oh, Tre! Yes, he and Lens were really close friends growing up. He moved here after Lens did and fell in love with Charleston."

"So Tre's from Atlanta?"

"Born and raised." Maya's expression grew sad. "Lens's death devastated him. He told me he had something special to perform last night, but I had no idea it was about Lens. The video I posted from last night is still getting engagement and likes."

"Do you think he'd be willing to talk on the podcast? "

Maya tilted her head. "He shouldn't mind. I'll definitely ask him. Who else will you be interviewing? I'm hoping after you publish this first episode, other people will come forward."

"Ace Clark is the only other person I have right now."

"Ace is perfect," Maya agreed. "I may need to coax her some, but you should interview Zara."

"Do you think Devante would be okay with his wife talking publicly about her relationship with Jerome?"

Maya's eyes flashed with anger, and her mouth opened as if she was about to say something. Then her face shuttered, becoming more composed. "Devante doesn't control Zara. She's her own woman, and she can make her own decisions about what she wants to share."

I wanted to ask more. I was curious how Zara ended up marrying their cousin. But Maya still looked flustered from dealing with her mom, and the Devante-Zara-Lens triangle appeared to be a touchy subject, so I decided to move on.

"Alright then," I said, adjusting my headphones. "If you're ready, I'll start the recording."

Maya squared her shoulders. "Let's do it."

I took a breath and pressed record.

COLD JUSTICE PODCAST

Season 4, Episode 1
Behind the Lens - The Sister

Published: June 9

JOSS: Welcome back to the *Cold Justice Podcast*. I'm your host, Joss Miller. For those of you who've been with me through our first three seasons, you know we strive to honor the victim. It's my hope loved ones will receive closure and possibly some answers from this podcast.

This season is once again centered in Charleston, South Carolina, but the victim held worldwide appeal on social media. Almost two years ago, a talented street photographer named Jerome McAbee, also known as "Lens," was found dead in the Charleston Harbor.

The official cause? Accidental drowning. Family members and friends have a hard time believing that was the case.

Lens's Instagram account continues to be maintained for people to enjoy his work. His last post gave the impression that Lens may have been trying to hint at something. Intrigued by that, we will get into thoughts from our guests this season.

Joining me today is online beauty influencer @MayaMac-Style. She will open up this discussion about her younger brother.

Maya, thank you for being here. I know this can't be easy.

MAYA: Thank you for having me, Joss. And thank you for being willing to look into this when everyone else has moved on.

JOSS: Before we discuss what happened to Lens, I'd like our listeners to know who he was. Can you tell us about your brother?

MAYA: [Deep breath] Jerome was fun, but he was also a deep person. Even his nickname, Lens, came from how he saw the world. Through a camera, yes, but also how he viewed people. He could find good in anything, anyone. He'd photograph the homeless, the forgotten, the overlooked, and somehow capture their dignity, their humanity.

JOSS: I've seen his work. It's powerful. And with over 100,000 followers on Instagram, it's obvious Lens captivated many.

MAYA: He didn't care about the followers, though. He cared about the stories behind the photos. He used to say, "Every face has a story that deserves to be seen."

JOSS: So powerful. Maya, tell us about your relationship with your brother.

MAYA: Our parents divorced when we were young. I'm not sure what happened, but I stayed with Mama, and Lens went with our father to live in Atlanta. It was hard on all of us.

Our father was an artist. He did acrylic paintings, so Lens grew up differently from me. Our dad gave him a lot more freedom than my mother gave me. Mama always felt like Dad exposed Lens to too much. He got into a bit of trouble, like most young men do when they're trying to find their way.

After our father died, Lens moved back to Charleston to be closer to family. I'm not sure where he picked up using the camera, but it spoke to his artistic side. He told me it saved him.

[Sniffles softly] I admired how he expressed himself through photography. His audience on social media grew really fast. He influenced and encouraged me to do my thing on social. [Sniffles] He always had my back.

JOSS: I'm so sorry. Do you want to take a minute?

MAYA: No, I'm fine. This is harder than I thought it would be.

JOSS: Let's talk about the night Lens died. The police report states he drowned near Pier 47 around 11 p.m. on June 13th. That was almost two years ago. What do you remember about that day?

MAYA: [Swallows] I actually hadn't talked to him that day. He'd been excited earlier that week. Said he was working on something different from his usual street photos.

I was getting started on my content creator gig. Beauty and fashion companies were blowing up my inbox all the time. You know how siblings are. We're doing our thing, so we don't keep in touch as regularly.

JOSS: So he didn't drop any hints about what he was working on? I imagine he backed up all his photos.

MAYA: You know what, that's right. He probably had cloud storage. [Laughs] I bet my brother probably took a million pictures.

JOSS: That is definitely something to look into. That would be a major task to take on.

MAYA: Like a needle in a haystack. I wouldn't know what to look for.

JOSS: The official report says he was taking photographs near the water and accidentally fell in. But you don't believe that.

MAYA: [On camera she shook her head, making her long earrings clap together.] Lens was terrified of deep water. Absolutely terrified. When we were kids, there was an incident at a public pool when he was seven. He nearly drowned, so he never went near deep water. Never. The idea that he'd be standing at the edge of a pier in the dark, alone, taking photos? Photos of what?

JOSS: His camera equipment was never recovered, right?

MAYA: That's the other thing. It's crazy that his backpack with his phone and camera were never found. Just his body. Lens's camera was expensive.

JOSS: Someone could have robbed him or taken it for other reasons. Did the police investigate those possibilities?

MAYA: When our family tried to push for more investigation, we were told there was no evidence other than it was an accident. The case was closed within a week. A week! They barely investigated at all.

I will say the detective on the case. She's a woman, can't think of her name right now. Now she agreed someone might have robbed Lens or maybe someone found the backpack.

JOSS: I'm familiar with the detective on the case. Detective Sara Wilkes. She has an excellent close rate for homicide cases. I guess evidence never arose suggesting foul play.

I want to turn attention to his last post on Instagram. For the listeners, let me read what he wrote: "The lens reveals what the heart refuses to see." You know what I found interesting was he posted a picture of himself which wasn't his normal post. He wasn't the type to do selfies, but always posted the subjects of his photos. From his statement, I expected to see a photograph of a place here in Charleston. What did you think about the post when you saw it?

MAYA: I think about that post every day. He posted it the morning he died. Lens was deliberate with his words. He was as much a poet as he was a photographer. That quote felt different from his usual posts—more personal, more painful. I kept wondering what his heart was refusing to see. Now I think maybe he found out something about someone he trusted, and it broke him.

JOSS: Maya, you came to me. What do you hope to accomplish by bringing Lens's story to the podcast?

MAYA: I want answers. My mama deserves to know what really happened to her son. They'd had such a rough relationship when he was younger, but those last few years... [voice breaking] they were finally healing. That's what makes this so hard. She finally got him back in her life, only to lose him forever. But more than that, if Lens died because he uncovered something, then his death can't be for nothing. I want to know what he was working on.

JOSS: Is there anything else you want our listeners to know about Lens?

MAYA: He wasn't another statistic, another young Black man gone too soon. He was a brother, a son, and an amazing artist. He deserved better than to have his death swept under the rug. He deserves justice.

JOSS: Thank you, Maya, for trusting me with Lens's story.

MAYA: Thank you for listening.

JOSS: Listeners, if you have any information about Lens or his activities in the days or even hours before his death, please reach out through our website.

Until then, I'm Joss Miller, and this is the *Cold Justice Podcast*.

Saturday, June 7 at 8:10 p.m.

I uploaded the final audio file and scheduled it to be published Monday morning. I laid across my bed, mentally exhausted. My usual roommate, one of the twin tuxedo cats in the house, Minnie, cuddled up beside me. Her deep purring soothed my aching head. Maya's voice still echoed in my ears. I'd had trouble editing the podcast; there were some portions I wasn't sure I wanted public.

Like the cloud storage... There had to be some evidence of what Lens had been working on. It was a shame that the investigation closed up so quickly. Maya didn't seem to have any type of access to her brother's digital footprint other than his Instagram account. He'd set her up as the one to take care of his account in case of his death.

I rubbed the top of Minnie's head and closed my eyes while replaying the interview in my mind. I don't know why, but certain details kept needling me.

Atlanta kept coming up. Lens had spent most of his childhood and teenage years there with his father.

Tre was from Atlanta and had followed Lens to Charleston.

My brother lived there doing undercover work.

Maya had been in Atlanta and ran into Nate.

I was so tired from the week that all these details became muddied in my head.

My eyes snapped open, and I jolted up, scaring the cat beside me. She eyed me warily, her body arched and ready to leap.

I mumbled, "Sorry," and reached for my MacBook. I wasn't sure why, but I wanted to know how Lance McAbee died. Maya had mentioned it so casually.

After our father died, Lens moved back to Charleston.

I opened a new browser tab and searched "Lance McAbee Atlanta artist death." My mouth fell open when I read the results.

Atlanta Artist Found Dead in Studio

Local artist Lance McAbee was found dead in his Midtown studio yesterday evening, the victim of an apparent robbery gone wrong. McAbee, known for his abstract paintings depicting urban life, was discovered by his son. Police say the studio had been ransacked and several paintings destroyed.

The investigation is ongoing.

I sat back, my mind racing. Lens's father had been murdered, and the case was unsolved.

And Lens had been the one to find his father. No wonder he left Atlanta.

I was about to search for follow-up articles when my phone rang. My mom's photo, a rare photo of her smiling, filled the screen. My father had captured the image when Mom was younger.

"Hey, Mom," I answered, still distracted by what I'd discovered.

"Joss, since Nate's here, I thought it would be nice to have dinner after church tomorrow."

I shut my laptop, forcing myself to focus on the conversation. "That sounds great." I paused. "Did Nate say how long he was staying?"

She hesitated slightly. "I haven't asked him."

"Mom, is everything okay with him? He seems different since he's been back." I was hoping she would tell me she and Nate talked about his career situation.

Mom's voice rose slightly. "Different how?"

Okay, maybe she still didn't know.

Come on, Nate!

"I don't know. Something seems to be bothering him. Haven't you noticed?"

My mom sucked in a breath. "Your brother is home. Let's be supportive, okay?"

I felt heat rise in my cheeks. I was being supportive, keeping Nate's DEA work secret from our mother. What would she think about her son being an undercover agent who'd been forced to flee Atlanta because his cover was blown?

My mom continued, as if exhausted from talking to me. "Joss, I want a nice Sunday dinner without any drama."

"Of course, Mom."

"Good, I'll see you tomorrow."

She hung up, and I stared at my phone for a long moment, feeling chastised. I'd always been a daddy's girl, and Nate was the apple of my mom's eyes. I knew his behavior over the past few years affected her as much as it did me. She was more interested in him being home now.

I reopened my MacBook and turned my attention back to the follow-up article about Lance McAbee's murder. The case had gone cold within months with no suspects identified.

In some ways, Lens's father's death, though different, felt similar to his son's death. Maya mentioned after Lens returned to Charleston, he seemed to handle his grief by picking up the camera.

Like Nate, returning home with his cover blown, had Lens come home to be with family, or had he been running from something that finally caught up with him?

Chapter 9

Spilling the Tea

Sunday, June 8 at 1:35 p.m.

My mother had plans for us, but her intentions morphed into a full family affair. My great aunts Ruth and Thelma wanted all of us to attend church and have Sunday dinner at their home. I knew my great aunts really wanted to get to know my brother. He'd met them briefly during the holidays, but they hadn't gotten to know him like my mom and me since he rarely visited over the years.

Mom was an adoptee, and the dynamics of our family changed once she decided to look for her biological parents. Her adoptive parents, Jonathan and Catherine Caldwell were already in their early forties when they adopted Mom. Grandpa Jonathan, a high school principal, passed away before Mom married Dad, so he had only been a man in photos to me and

Nate. I had some solid memories of Nana spoiling us before she died during my freshman year in high school.

After Nana's death, Mom told us that she'd been adopted. Dad had encouraged Mom to take a DNA test and begin the search for her biological parents. Several DNA matches from distant cousins led her to her biological father's family first.

August Manning, Mom's biological father, had been killed long before she was born. His brutal death was the subject of my first podcast season. His sisters, Ruth and Thelma accepted my mother and our family with open arms, especially since neither had married or had children of their own. The aunts told Mom the story of August's ill-fated relationship with Louise, a young white woman.

The day my mom visited the Hopkins's home, she never got to meet Louise. Louise's now deceased husband turned Mom away. For years, my mom thought Louise had rejected her. While their relationship had improved, I connected more with Louise than my mother. I think I missed having a "Nana" in my life. Dad and Mom were only children. After dad died, our family circle became even smaller. I cherished our newly expanded family.

Aunt Ruth and Aunt Thelma outdid themselves with Sunday dinner. Aunt Ruth wore a bright red, frilly apron over her church dress, while her sister donned a floral apron with large purple flowers over hers. The fried chicken glistened from the center of the table, but my stomach was pining for my favorite, mac and cheese. I looked over at Nate's wide eyes. Our mother didn't do this type of cooking. It felt like Christmas in June.

Aunt Thelma carried a cast-iron skillet with oven mitts. "Okay, we almost have everything. Here's the cornbread. Ruth, you got the greens?"

Aunt Ruth followed, "Yes, here they go." She set the large porcelain bowl of steaming greens next to the chicken.

Mom shook her head. "Y'all always cook so much food."

Aunt Ruth grinned. "Well, we don't get to cook for family often." She gestured toward Nate with her serving spoon. "We're so happy to see you. I was telling Thelma when you were here last Christmas how much you reminded me of August."

I looked at my brother. A resemblance to our grandfather never occurred to me. I'd inherited my looks from my dad, and Nate had some of mom's features. But looking back and forth between the portrait of our grandfather on the dining room wall and my brother, I could see the similarities around the eyes and their shared deep brown complexion.

Nate glanced up at the portrait. "I wish I'd known him."

Aunt Ruth sighed. "We miss him every day. Let's bow our heads for grace." As the oldest sister and oldest living member of the Manning family, Aunt Ruth led us in prayer with her soothing voice.

We filled up the aunts' good china plates with the offerings. For a few minutes, mouths smacking and utensils clinking filled the room.

Then Aunt Thelma turned to Nate. "Your mama said you live in Atlanta. What do you do that keeps you so busy?"

I caught Nate's slight hesitation as he buttered his cornbread. "Consulting work mostly. Different companies, different projects."

With what I knew about my brother's life, that lie slipped too easily off his tongue. Made me wonder about his life undercover. How many people had he fooled with his fake persona?

Thelma nodded, but her slight frown said she didn't really understand.

"How long you planning to stay in Charleston?" Aunt Ruth asked.

"I'm not sure yet," Nate replied. "Depends on a few things."

Aunt Thelma tried again. "That's an interesting job. Sounds like you have some say in your time at work. Is that consulting work like an entrepreneur or something?"

Nate wiped his mouth with his napkin. "Something like that. It keeps me pretty busy." He glanced at me. I couldn't help myself. I raised an eyebrow at him, kind of happy our great aunts had him sweating.

Even though Mom and I helped clear the table, Aunt Ruth and Aunt Thelma insisted on helping with the cleanup, so I left the women and went to find Nate. He'd escaped to the back porch, his solid frame snug in a wooden rocking chair. I settled into one of the rocking chairs next to him.

On the other side of the porch, our aunts had a small vegetable garden with tomatoes, cucumbers and a neat row of collard greens.

"Don't you love them? I wish we had known them growing up."

Nate patted his flat stomach. "Definitely didn't have meals like that at Nana's house."

I shrugged. "She tried. Mom said she wasn't much of a cook. But Mom does okay. She makes some good dishes sometimes." I thought I should let my brother know about the podcast since my first guest was his ex-girlfriend. "I interviewed Maya yesterday for the podcast."

Nate whipped his head around. "You're going through with that story?"

I eyed him. "Yeah. It's about time for me to take on a new cold case. And I'm interested in what really happened to Lens. Did you know him? I never knew Maya had a brother."

Nate leaned forward in the chair. "I met him a few times when he was in town. He lived in Atlanta with their dad."

"Did you meet Maya's dad?"

He nodded. "A few times when he and Maya's brother came to town, usually during the summer or the holidays."

"Did you know Maya's dad was murdered?"

Nate turned and stared at me. "How do you know, and what does that have to do with your podcast?"

"It interested me. She mentioned his death so casually. I guess the distance kept them from being close. Anyway, I do my research for these podcasts, and I looked him up since I knew he was also an artist. Could be me overthinking, but I felt like there were some similarities between how the father and the son died."

Nate was quiet for a long moment. "Joss, you need to be really careful with this one."

I frowned. "What do you mean?"

He glanced around, making sure we were still alone on the porch. "Let's just say that Lens wasn't just a street photographer taking pretty pictures. Word was he'd gotten mixed up with some dangerous people in Atlanta."

"Mixed up how?"

"I can't give you specifics, but..." Nate rubbed his face with his hands. "The kind of people I investigate don't like having their pictures taken, if you know what I mean."

My heart started racing. "Are you saying Lens was photographing drug dealers?"

"I'm saying Jerome was in the wrong place at the wrong time more than once. And people in that business have a way of making problems disappear." Nate took a deep breath, then he leaned back, and started rocking again. "You got to cool it with these amateur investigations. Haven't you gotten yourself in some hot water with these podcasts before?"

"Yes, but I know to be careful." I peered at him, hoping he wouldn't shut down on me with my next question. "The other night when Maya said you ignored her..."

Nate's rocking slowed. "Joss—"

I glanced behind me before leaning toward him. "If you were undercover and Maya recognized you... Did she blow your cover?"

My brother stopped rocking entirely, his hands gripped the armrests of the chair. For a long moment, he stared out at the garden, his jaw working like he was trying to decide how much to tell me.

"You really are too smart for your own good," he said finally.

"I'm sorry. Maya and I talked about her dad and brother living in Atlanta, and it occurred to me that you and her might have crossed paths. You both were in Atlanta too."

He sighed. "Atlanta is a big city. But yes, we ended up at the same club. Maya saw me across the room and..." He ran his hands through his hair. "She called out my name a few times. I ignored her, but then she came right up to me and grabbed my arm."

My heart sank. "Oh no."

"Damage was done. The woman I was with was not pleased about this other woman trying to get my attention. I told her she'd been mistaken, thought I was someone else."

I didn't miss the fact my brother mentioned he'd been at this club with a woman. I wondered what role this other woman had in his life. Was he serious about her or was she someone he was with as a part of his cover? "Is that why you had to leave Atlanta?"

He nodded grimly. "Among other things. I'm supposed to be out of town for business. I didn't want to leave; I felt like it made me look more suspicious. But to be on the safe side, I followed orders from my SAC."

I peered at my brother. "Um, what's a SAC?"

Nate chuckled. "Sorry. That's short for Special Agent in Charge. Anyway, I'm hoping to go back once they set up a sting operation. That could be any day now."

I felt a surge of anger toward Maya, even though she couldn't have known what she was doing. If Nate was there with another woman, what possessed her to call him out like that? "Does Maya know? About your job?"

He shook his head. "Typical Maya wanting attention, and I don't know why. She was there with that guy from the other night who performed at your Friday Night Jam."

"Tre Kennedy? Oh yeah, Maya mentioned he was Lens's friend in Atlanta." I sighed. "I'm so sorry your cover was blown."

The screen door creaked open behind us. Mom's voice rang out, tight with concern. "What is Joss talking about? Your cover was blown! What does that mean?"

Sunday, June 8 at 3:24 p.m.

Nate and I both shot up from the rocking chairs, making the chairs thump against the porch boards in a chaotic rhythm. Mom stood in the doorway, her eyes darting from Nate to me, and then she glared at Nate. My stomach churned as I glanced at my brother, wondering how much of our conversation Mom heard.

Nate's shoulders rose as if preparing for battle. He spoke slowly, "Mom—"

She stepped onto the porch, jabbing her finger in his direction. "Don't 'Mom' me, Nathan David Miller. What kind of cover? What were you talking about?" Her voice rose with each word. "And, Joss, how do you know about this when I don't?"

My stomach dropped at hearing my mom say my brother's whole government name. It startled me to hear his middle name, the same as our father's first name. I stuttered. "I just found out."

"Of course you did!" Mom's eyes blazed. "No one tells me anything. How did I raise two children who don't know how to talk to me?"

"Clarice, honey." Aunt Ruth's gentle voice came from behind Mom as she and Aunt Thelma appeared in the doorway.

"What's all this shouting about? The neighbors are going to think we're having a family feud out here."

"We don't need no one calling the police on us." Aunt Thelma clasped her hands together in front of her. "Why don't we all come inside for some apple pie?"

"That sounds like a good idea." Aunt Ruth headed in our direction.

Mom looked ready to explode, but as soon as Aunt Ruth placed her hand on Mom's back, she wilted, letting the older woman guide her back inside.

Beside me, Nate muttered, "This is why I've stayed away. She blows up over everything."

Here I thought it was just me.

Our mother had a hot and cold button. Sometimes she left you out in the freezing cold with silence. Other times her anger burned you, leaving you feeling crispy for days, sometimes months, afterwards. Dad was neither. We knew when we disappointed him, but his emotions always stayed stable. In fact, he would warn us not to upset our mother. I thought my brother had taken that piece of advice a little too far this time.

We all filed back into the dining room. In the center of the table was a flaky, golden apple pie. Aunt Ruth passed around small white china plates with forks, while Aunt Thelma cut generous slices.

One of them had placed some Cool Whip on the table. I grabbed it and swirled out a nice lump on top of my pie slice. I noticed Nate and Mom were staring at their plates. I dug into mine, grateful for something that would help me ignore the mounting tension.

"Alright." Mom's jaw worked as if she was trying to maintain control. "Someone better start explaining. Now."

Nate took a deep breath. "I work for the DEA, Mom. I've been undercover for the past year and a half investigating drug trafficking operations. That's why I've been so distant. I couldn't tell you where I was or what I was doing."

"DEA? Undercover?" Mom's voice cracked. "You've been working with... with criminals?"

"Investigating them," Nate corrected gently. "But, yes, it means I have to maintain a cover identity. I can't have regular contact with family because it could put you in danger or compromise the operation."

Aunt Ruth stared wide eyed at Nate. "Oh, my Lord. That explains why you've been so secretive."

"And now your cover's been compromised?" Mom's voice was an octave higher than usual.

Nate nodded. "Maya—" He explained to both aunts. "My ex-girlfriend...she recognized me and made a scene at an inconvenient time. I had to leave Atlanta until the department could set up a sting operation to take down the organization I infiltrated."

Mom sat back in her chair, her shoulders sagged. "This is... this is a lot to process. I've always wondered what exactly you were doing with this consultant thing. Why it kept you so busy that you couldn't stay in touch and come home more often? You're in law enforcement. This is worse than your sister and her podcast hobby."

I placed my fork down on my empty plate. "Wait a minute. Podcasting is not a hobby! In fact, a new season of the *Cold Justice Podcast* starts tomorrow about Maya's brother, Lens —Jerome McAbee. He was a photographer who died under suspicious circumstances here in Charleston."

My mom rolled her eyes so hard, all we saw were the whites of her eyes. When she finished her dramatic eye gymnastics, she stared at me. "You're kidding me. I thought you would tire of that podcast. Are you asking for someone to come after you again?"

I didn't know what to say, so I stared down at my plate. Mom had never completely supported the podcast. And she often reminded me of last summer's ordeal, like I needed reminding.

Aunt Ruth patted our mother's hand. "Your children are doing good things. They're helping bring some justice to this world."

Mom spoke with a shaky voice. "I guess you both get it from your father. David Miller always loved his mysteries and true crime shows. He'd read detective novels and watch those investigation programs for hours. I got the impression if he could live his life over, he would have chosen law enforcement instead of being an accountant."

Her voice broke. "If he was alive today, I guess he would love this for both of you. But I'm not like him. I don't like this. Joss is publicly investigating murder cases. Now I find out my son is risking his life with drug dealers."

"Both of your children are smart and capable," Aunt Thelma added, "and you've got the Lord watching over them."

"That's right," Aunt Ruth nodded. "Thelma and I are always praying for all of you."

Nate held up his hands as if surrendering. "Mom, I'm sorry I couldn't tell you before. But I promise you, I'm careful. I have good training, and there are people looking out for me."

For a long moment, Mom didn't say anything. Then she shook her head. "What now? Are you in danger, Nate?"

He shrugged. "I left Atlanta under the guise of going on a business trip. All I can do is wait for my instructions on next steps."

She frowned and looked at me. "You said you're investigating Maya's brother's death." She shook her head. "I didn't even know Maya had a brother."

"He lived with their father in Atlanta." Nate looked at me. "Why are you investigating his death? I know Maya is still grieving, but the man drowned."

"Yes, but..." I wasn't sure how much to say. My great aunts, mom, and Nate were all looking at me. "Look, the family and some friends don't believe he drowned by accident. My podcast is out there for people to talk. Maybe someone knows something. Andre said that even Detective Wilkes thought something was up with his death."

Mom placed her hand over her head. "Are you going to promise me you'll be careful?"

"Always," I said. "I'm not taking unnecessary risks. Besides, I have Andre. He always has my back."

She sighed deeply. "Poor Andre. I guess it's only love that he puts up with you."

"Of course." I grinned.

My mom gave me a small smile back. The storm had subsided for now. She picked up her fork and dug into her pie. "I don't like any of this. I'm an accountant who deals with numbers. Numbers are safe. But I suppose I'd rather know what my adult children are doing instead of wondering."

"And now we can all pray specifically for what you both need." Aunt Thelma placed her hands together on top of the table. "Protection for Nate in his work, wisdom for Joss in her investigation, and peace for you, Clarice, as their mother."

"So," Aunt Ruth said, cutting herself another small slice of pie, "Joss, tell us about your young man. Why isn't he here and when is he going to put a ring on that finger?"

I gulped.

Chapter 10
Full Steam Ahead

Monday, June 9 at 9:15 a.m.

The first episode with Maya dropped at midnight. My phone had been pinging all morning thanks to Maya tagging me in her early morning reel. I couldn't believe she really woke up and made her face up to appear on camera that early. Once I arrived at work and chatted with Fay, I placed my phone in my locker to ignore the notifications.

Today, I was back working in the café. Even though I enjoyed the camp last week, it felt good to be around customers and serving up orders.

"One vanilla latte and a cranberry muffin." I set the tray on the table in front of Eleanor, who arrived bright and early with her laptop.

Our resident author beamed at me. "Thank you, Joss. I saw your post about the new podcast episode this morning. I haven't listened yet, but I saw you had a ton of downloads."

"Yes, the first episode kicked off well this morning, thanks to my guest. She's the victim's sister." I gestured to her laptop. "What are you working on these days?"

Eleanor tapped the top of her laptop. "A new cozy mystery series. It's still coming together. I need to send a proposal to my agent this week."

"Well, I can't wait to hear more. Let me head back." By the time I situated myself behind the counter, the door chimed. I looked up to see Andre walking in. My heart did that little skip it always did when I saw him. We hadn't seen each other in a few days, but I kept him updated with our nightly phone calls. I'd told him about the family drama between Mom and Nate, but I purposely left off my aunts' inquiry about a marriage proposal.

"Good morning, Joss." He said, approaching the counter. Though he was smiling, I could tell by the small bags under his eyes, he'd had quite the weekend.

"Morning. Black coffee?" I asked, already reaching for a cup. Fay didn't seem to mind that my boyfriend got coffee on the house. She did the same thing for her boyfriend. The plumber always showed up at the café as if we had plumbing issues, when he really came to check on his sweetie, Fay.

"You know me too well." He leaned against the counter as I poured the steaming java. "How are you holding up after yesterday?"

"I'm good. Not sure how my brother is feeling today."

Andre shrugged. "I'm sure he's relieved to get that weight off his chest. Your mom needs time to process. She accepted your podcast."

I handed him his coffee, letting my fingers brush against his. "I don't know about that, but at least she knows about the new season. The first episode is getting a lot of traffic."

He took a sip before placing the cup on the counter. I could tell by the way he narrowed his eyes that he was about to switch into detective mode.

"Uh oh. I'm in trouble."

He crossed his arms. "Not yet, but Detective Wilkes asked me about your choice of topic for the podcast this morning. I take it she listened to it."

My heart leaped in my chest. I'd had run-ins with Detective Wilkes in the past. I wasn't trying to show up in an interrogation room with her ever again.

I mumbled, "That can't be good!"

Andre placed his hands on the counter and leaned in. "I know I can't stop you from investigating, and I've learned not to try. But if you learn something, Detective Wilkes will want to know immediately."

I blew out a breath. "Of course. I appreciate that she hasn't given up on the case."

He reached for his cup. "Wilkes doesn't like to have cold cases. It messes with her solid close rate."

Before I could respond, Ace came through the café door.

I raised an eyebrow. "Hey, Ace. I thought you were off today."

"I'm working across the street with my mom today." Ace's mom owned an insurance company. He still took photos of properties for her.

Ace held out his fist for a dap. "Hey, Detective Baez."

Andre returned the gesture. "Ace, my man. Good to see you working hard."

"Trying to. Hey, Joss, I've been checking socials all morning. People are talking about Lens." He turned to Andre. "I'm going to be on the next episode. I can't wait to tell people what Lens was really like, and what he was working on."

Andre's jaw tightened slightly. "Did Detective Wilkes talk to you?"

Ace shook his head. "The police never came to see me, even though I was a close friend."

"Really?" Andre glanced at me. "Remember to be careful about what you share publicly. Sometimes the wrong people pay attention to these things."

Ace's face sobered. "I hadn't thought about it that way."

"It's not a problem. I will edit the audio. If anything comes up I don't think should be out there, it won't be in the final episode. And I can pass it along to Wilkes."

"Good." Andre finished his coffee. "I need to head into work. I'll catch up with you later." He blew me a kiss, and I unabashedly caught it and blew one back.

After Andre left, Ace shook his head. "You guys are really in love."

I grinned. "Yes, we are." I reached under the counter and grabbed a towel. Ace followed me as I started wiping down tables.

"I know you're going to edit the podcast, but do you really think someone might come after us? You know, for talking."

"I think Andre's right. We should be cautious," I said. "Do you want to back out?"

Ace shook his head. "No way!" He glanced around. "After talking to Maya yesterday, I may have something."

My senses tingled. I looked around the café, realizing it was probably not a good idea for us to be talking so openly, but I didn't see anyone in particular that concerned me.

Then the door chimed, and the person who walked in looked like he was looking for trouble.

Monday, June 9 at 10:05 a.m.

Devante sauntered into the café. One of the newer baristas, Kia Winters, practically bounced up to the counter. She was a college sophomore working on her communications degree. Petite with a gleaming smile, she'd mentioned her goal was to be a news anchor. I admired how she greeted each customer with enthusiasm.

"Hey, welcome to Sugar Creek Café. Can I take your order?"

Devante didn't even acknowledge Kia. Instead, his intense brown eyes scanned the café until they landed on me and Ace. His jaw tightened when he saw us together.

I slid a look toward Ace, knowing he didn't like Devante.

"Joss," Devante's eyes bore into me, ignoring Ace.

Hoping I could deescalate whatever was bothering this man, I smiled. "Hey, Devante. How are things going? I appreciate you teaching at the camp last week."

I must have caught him off guard. For a brief second, his face went blank. "I enjoyed it." But he recovered quickly and narrowed his eyes. "Look, I listened to your podcast today."

"What did you think?" I didn't really want to know, but I would keep an open mind.

Devante's eyes flickered to Ace then back to me. "I think Maya wants the attention."

I stepped back, a bit stunned. "What? Maya is seeking closure for her and her family."

His laugh was bitter. "Closure? Maya didn't even like her brother. They never got along. She wants the status her brother had on social media."

"No." Ace blurted. "You were the one jealous of Lens."

Devante locked eyes with Ace. "Is that what he told you?"

I turned around and noticed the café had grown quiet. Kia gawked at us from behind the counter, looking like she was ready to flee. All we needed was for Fay to come out of her office. "Okay, guys. You both need to cool it, or my boss is going to throw you both out."

Devante's shoulders slumped.

As Hailey had mentioned last week, I noted he still wasn't wearing a wedding ring. With what I learned this past weekend, I decided to test the waters. "I met your wife at Friday Night Jam. Zara seemed really nice."

Devante clenched his hands at his sides. "She told me she was going out with friends."

Ace and I exchanged a quick glance.

"Well, she came with Maya. They seem to be good friends."

"Maya." He practically spat her name. "Of course. She's been filling Zara's head with all kinds of nonsense about Lens. Making her think she needs to 'honor his memory' or whatever Maya thinks she's doing."

"She was his girlfriend first." Ace tossed in.

Devante's head snapped toward him. He looked ready to say something, but then I heard the melodious voice of my boss behind me.

"Joss, is everything okay? Ace, honey, you're supposed to be off." Fay's voice was soothing, but when I spun around, I could tell she was concerned. Her narrowed eyes focused on Devante.

I couldn't blame her. Wound tight like a snake ready to strike, Devante's intensity radiated off of him. Gruffly he stated, "I need to go."

As quickly as he arrived, Devante exited the café, leaving me with a lot of questions.

I watched Devante stalk down the sidewalk through the café's front window. It occurred to me that I wasn't even sure why he showed up. Did he come to the café just to let me know he wasn't pleased about the podcast? If so, why was he so against it? Seeing his reaction to Zara being out with Maya on Friday, I wondered if this was more about his marriage than anything else.

Chapter 11

Espresso Revelations

Monday, June 9 at 6:45 p.m.

The two afternoon baristas were helping Fay close tonight, so I left the café early. It gave me time to prepare for tonight's recording session with Ace. After our conversation earlier, I was more eager than ever to get his perspective on record. As Lens's close friend, Ace might know details that Detective Wilkes missed during her original investigation.

Andre always praised Wilkes's exceptional solve rate for homicide cases, but even the best detectives could overlook something when a case seemed straightforward. Now that I knew Wilkes was paying attention to the podcast, I wanted to make sure I got all the facts right. If *Cold Justice Podcast* could provide new information that led to reopening Lens's case, it would be worth every risk.

I pulled into the driveway and cut the engine. Sometimes I liked to sit in the car for a few moments to get my thoughts together before heading inside and giving my grandmother my full attention. Right now, I couldn't stop thinking about Devante's reaction earlier.

Why would he think Maya was just wanting attention? And even if she didn't get along with her brother, that didn't mean she didn't love him or wouldn't want to know what happened to him. My brother certainly had annoyed me over the years, but I was happy he was here in Charleston and that his secrets were out.

What really struck me was how Devante's face changed when I mentioned Zara being at Friday Night Jam. I'd seen that possessive look before on past boyfriends. Like you weren't supposed to do anything without them. But then he wasn't wearing a wedding ring. What was that about?

I definitely saw where Ace was coming from. Devante wasn't who he seemed. The guy who helped young kids learn about photography and took stunning wedding portraits also had a different side to him.

My grandmother was in her usual spot in her chair with the orange tabby, Ginger, curled up in her lap. I could see the nightly news report playing on the television.

My grandmother smiled. "Joss, how was your day?"

"Not too bad." I dropped my purse on the floor and sank down on the couch. "The new podcast episode is doing even better than expected." I was truly grateful since I never knew how the first episode was going to go, especially since I take so many months in between seasons.

Louise muted the television and turned to face me. "That's wonderful, dear. And how is your brother doing? Do you think he will come by to see me?"

Yesterday, I'd thought about inviting Louise to Sunday dinner at Ruth and Thelma's house. My great-aunts wouldn't have minded. They'd always been fond of Louise. But my mother still had her issues with her biological mother. The last thing we needed yesterday was more family drama besides Nate's secret life.

I said carefully. "Things are complicated right now."

Louise studied my face. "I see. He seems to be a lot like your mother."

I tilted my head. "You can say that." I wasn't sure if I could even mention what had happened yesterday without Nate's permission. Knowing my mother, she wouldn't like Louise knowing. And too many people already knew about Nate's situation.

Funny how easy it was to keep secrets.

I stood. "I'm going to head upstairs and get ready for another recording session."

Louise raised an eyebrow. "Another one? So soon."

"I want to get another episode out this week." I hoped the combination of Maya and Ace's episodes would bring others out to talk.

"Well, make sure you eat something before you get started. Eugeena brought us some ribs, corn on the cob and potato salad. The Pattersons and Jones had a feast yesterday."

Eugeena Patterson-Jones had been my grandmother's next-door neighbor for decades. She and her husband Amos always looked out for Louise, whether it was cutting her grass or making sure she ate a good meal. I'd received some benefits from that neighborly friendship, too.

"I'm so glad you have them next door."

Louise chuckled. "Me too. Thank you for bringing me some of Thelma's apple pie. We never have to worry about starving around here."

"Nope." Not being much of a cook, I was grateful.

I went upstairs and took a shower. Then returned to the kitchen to enjoy my second day of eating some down home cooking. I certainly couldn't eat like this every day. With my

STEAMY ESPRESSO SECRETS

belly satisfied, I checked on my grandmother, who was already asleep for the evening. When she moved back into her home after a brief stint in the nursing home.

With the house quiet, I tiptoed upstairs, careful to step over Minnie and Mickey. For whatever reason, the two tuxedo cats enjoyed hanging out on the staircase until bedtime.

By the time I logged into the Zoom call, Ace was already in the lobby. "Oh, you're early, Ace. And I didn't know you wore glasses."

Ace touched the black square frames. "Oh yeah, I try to give my eyes a break from the contacts at night." His eyes widened behind the frames. "I'm kind of nervous after the warning from Detective Baez."

I giggled. "No need to be nervous. You're having a conversation with a friend. But before we dive into the interview, let's talk. It will get you feeling more comfortable."

"Sure." Ace sat back in what appeared to be one of those tall gaming chairs.

"I have to ask you about what happened today with Devante. Tell me about Lens and Zara's relationship. Were you around them both?"

Ace adjusted his glasses. "Lens really loved Zara. Like, really loved her. He was saving up for a ring, always talking about proposing. Said she was the one person who understood his work, his passion for documenting the community."

"And she felt the same way?"

"That's what I thought. I mean, they had J.J."

"J.J? Wait, Lens had a kid with Zara?"

Ace nodded. "He's about four years old now."

"I didn't know that. He never showed his personal life on Instagram."

Ace hesitated. "Lens had a private account. Only a few people had access. It's hard to believe Zara is with Devante now."

"Do you think something was going on between Zara and Devante? Maybe Lens found out."

"I don't know. I will say, looking back, that Zara could be awkward when Devante was around at like family events. I assumed that was because Lens and Devante flat out didn't like each other."

"They were cousins."

Ace shrugged. "Yeah, but they didn't grow up around each other. Remember, Lens grew up in Atlanta."

I thought about that for a minute. "And Zara is from Charleston?"

Ace nodded his head. "Yes."

"So would she have known Devante first?"

Ace's eyes widened. "Are you trying to say maybe Lens is the one who stole the girl?"

"That might explain some of the animosity between the two cousins."

Ace closed his eyes as if he didn't want to accept that revelation about his friend and mentor.

I jotted notes in my notebook. I was definitely seeing some patterns here. Might even explain why Devante seemed so uptight. But how much did Devante not like his cousin?

"I heard that Zara was one of the last people Lens talked to before he died. So if they had a son, I'm assuming they lived together."

Ace rubbed his head. "Yeah. She was the one who called the police and reported him missing. She had to go to work, and it was unlike Lens to not return to the house to watch their son. She said they argued that night and Lens left the house. Lens was a person who didn't like conflict and arguing about stuff."

"Did she share what the argument was about? Maybe Lens shared something with you when y'all were talking."

Ace shook his head. "As far as I could tell, Lens had nothing but love for her."

I really wanted to talk to Zara. Would she be candid about her last hours with Lens?

"Ace, since you and Lens were close friends, did you know about what happened to Lens's dad?"

Ace's thick eyebrows furrowed together as he pushed his glasses closer up his nose. "That's a random question."

"I did a lot of research. It helps me to know more about him."

He nodded. "Makes sense. All I know is Len's father was killed in his Atlanta studio. The police never found who did it. After his death, Lens moved to Charleston. I guess he wanted to get away from Atlanta."

"Did he have any ideas about who may have wanted to hurt his father?"

"I don't know. I know it bothered him." Ace licked his lips. "Why are you asking about Lens's dad?"

"Just some theories. Can't have a true crime podcast without having some theories. I wondered what Lens was looking into before his death. If I was in his shoes, I may have wanted to investigate my father's death."

Ace appeared confused. "Yeah, I hear you, but that happened in Atlanta. Like I said, Lens moved here to get away."

I crossed my arms, leaning my elbows on my desk. "To get away from what or whom?"

Ace was quiet for a long moment. "That's a good point. And I don't know if you knew this, but Lens went to Atlanta a few weeks before he died."

I leaned closer to my MacBook. "Really? Did you notice if he was different when he came back?"

Ace hesitated. "Yea, he was kind of different."

My pulse quickened, and I scribbled a note down in my notebook. "I might want to get more into that on the interview, in case other people noticed the same thing. Will you be comfortable talking about it?"

"Yeah, sure."

"Now, before we get started, you said you had something that might be interesting after talking to Maya. What's that about?"

"Oh yeah, Maya said you asked her about whether Lens backed up his photos. Of course he did. That's what makes it so crazy that the police decided he drowned. You're talking about looking at his photos on his feed. What if there were some photos he hadn't posted yet? I've gone out with him when he used to take photos. Lens took hundreds of photos. And, I know where he kept them."

Ace was full of information this evening, and we hadn't even started the interview yet. "How do you know?"

He pushed his glasses up his nose. "We actually shared a Google Drive account when we started a YouTube channel together about a year before he died. Nothing big, but I thought it would be cool for Lens to get more into video, documenting Charleston street art and local musicians. Lens was more interested in the cinematography, and I handled the editing."

"I didn't know you two had a YouTube account. Can you share it?"

Ace nodded. "Sure. The YouTube channel never really took off like we hoped, but Lens had been using the Google Drive for his photos. I didn't realize he'd been paying for it until I saw emails about the Google One storage plan needing a new payment option. When I saw how much he had stored, I added my card. I keep meaning to download everything to an external drive."

"Wow! You have access to all his photos." I tried to keep the excitement out of my voice.

Ace shrugged. "I never really dug through his personal folders after he died. It felt wrong, you know? But after talking to Maya today about cloud storage, I peeked through some folders."

My heart raced. "Did you see anything? There might be something we can share with the police. If we can get the case reopened, that would be a big deal."

"There were a lot of folders. Lots of photos." Ace glanced around his room as if someone was listening or looking over his shoulder. "I don't want to get us in trouble."

"My goal is to keep us out of trouble." A quick look at the time made me nervous. "It's getting late. Do you feel comfortable enough for me to record and start the interview?"

He nodded. "Are you going to ask me questions about the cloud storage?"

"Definitely not. That's not for public knowledge."

But I was eager to see what he found.

COLD JUSTICE PODCAST

Season 4, Episode 2
Behind the Lens - The Friend
Published: June 10

JOSS: Welcome back to the *Cold Justice Podcast*. I'm Joss Miller. This is episode two of our investigation into the death of Jerome McAbee, a Charleston street photographer known as "Lens" to family and friends. Last week, we heard from Lens's sister Maya about the man behind the camera and why she believes his death was no accident.

Today, I'm speaking with another local photographer, Ace Clark, who was also a close friend of Lens. Ace, welcome to the podcast.

ACE: Thanks, Joss. I appreciate you doing this. Lens deserves to have his story told.

JOSS: Lens was older than you. How did you two become friends?

ACE: I was sixteen, taking photos with my phone at a street festival. Pretty rough time in my life. Lens saw me trying to photograph this saxophone player, and he walked up and said, "You're standing in the wrong spot. The story isn't in his face, it's in his hands." He spent the next few hours giving me impromptu lessons about finding the real story in a scene.

JOSS: How sweet! So Lens became your mentor and a friend. The police report mentions Lens's camera was never recovered. Being a photographer yourself, can you explain why that's significant?

ACE: [Slight pause] Lens used a Canon 5D Mark IV with an L-series lens. We're talking about eight thousand dollars' worth of equipment. [Reaches off-camera] Hold on, let me show you something.

[He holds up a red protective case.] This is my camera case. It's the same brand Lens used. As you can see, mine is red. Lens's camera case was yellow. He used to joke that it was like "caution tape." You could spot it from across the street.

As a street photographer, Lens was constantly moving through different neighborhoods. These cases aren't for show. I'm about to sound like a commercial, but they're impact-resistant, weatherproof, the whole deal. Photographers are paranoid about protecting our gear. These are big investments.

Now imagine this thing in a waterproof backpack. [Ace holds up a black backpack.] Lens had a bright blue backpack similar to this one. Even if Lens had somehow fallen in that water with his camera, his bright yellow case should have floated on the surface. And his backpack should have been nearby.

JOSS: This was pretty late at night. What could he have possibly been taking photos of that night?

ACE: Exactly. That's the other thing that doesn't make sense. Light was an important part of Lens's craft. He loved the whole art form of cinematography. Yeah, he had a flash on his phone, but I imagine he would only have been near the water during sunset or sunrise. He taught me a lot about using natural light to capture your subject.

JOSS: Let's talk about that last week. When did you last see Lens?

ACE: The weekend before he died. I was at his son's birthday party. J.J. turned two years old. [laughs] There were a lot more adults at that party than kids.

JOSS: How did Lens feel about being a dad?

ACE: Lens loved being a dad. He'd been taking pictures of J.J. since the day he was born, said he wanted his son to see how much he was loved.

JOSS: Who else was at the party?

ACE: His whole family was there. Maya, of course. Zara. Um, she was still his girlfriend then. Lens's mom, Caroline, a few neighborhood kids. But like I said, it was more adults. Lens's friend, Tre Kennedy, was there. His cousin Devante Cavanaugh.

JOSS: Anything different about him before his death?

ACE: [paused] I noticed something but didn't really pay it much attention until after I found out he died. That should have been a happy day, you know? Lens had a way of being the life of any party. He took photos like usual, always had his camera around his neck. But he barely smiled.

JOSS: Was there anything specific that happened at the party?

ACE: Well, I remember Devante and Lens stepped outside to talk privately. When they came back in, Lens looked...I don't know...shaken? And Devante left pretty soon after that.

JOSS: Did Lens say anything about what they discussed?

ACE: No, and I didn't want to pry. It was J.J.'s birthday, you know?

JOSS: Interesting. So me and you talked a bit before this recording. You said Lens traveled back to Atlanta, where he grew up. Was this before the birthday party?

ACE: Yeah, he'd gotten back a few days before his son's party. To be honest, he'd been subdued since that trip.

JOSS: Did Lens mention why he went to Atlanta?

ACE: I think he went to support Tre Kennedy. He's a spoken word artist who does shows all around the Southeast.

JOSS: That's right. They're good friends. Both from Atlanta.

ACE: They went to high school together.

JOSS: I recently learned about Lens's dad, Lance McAbee. He was also an artist. For folks who are listening to this podcast, Lens's dad was killed about seven years ago. Lens moved back to Charleston after his father's death. I found it interesting that his dad's murder also remains unsolved.

ACE: Me and Lens talked about it sometimes. I know it bothered him.

JOSS: I want to ask you a similar question that I asked Lens's sister earlier this week. What did you think of Lens's last Instagram post? "The lens reveals what the heart refuses to see."

ACE: Like I said earlier, Lens was the life of the party. But something was bothering him. I know he had a project that he was working on, but he seemed disappointed and sad.

JOSS: I'm really sorry, Ace. I know he was a close friend and mentor to you. Is there anything else you want our listeners to know?

ACE: Just... Lens saw the world differently than most people. For example, while people come to Charleston to take pictures of Rainbow Row and historic mansions, he documented the real city. The hard working folks trying to make a living, the people being pushed out, and the communities being erased.

JOSS: Thank you, Ace. Listeners, I encourage you to add your feedback to this episode through our website or social media.

Until then, I'm Joss Miller, and this is the *Cold Justice Podcast*.

Chapter 12

Bubbling Discoveries

Tuesday, June 10 at 12:29 a.m.

I probably should have waited a few days, but I published episode two at midnight. I felt like Ace and I had touched on some good topics. I could have been grasping at straws, bringing up Lens's dad's death. I found it interesting that Ace noticed a change in Lens after his trip to Atlanta.

Lately, Chocolate City had been coming up a good bit in conversation. Which reminded me I hadn't heard from my brother or mother since Sunday. Since Nate was staying at our childhood home, hopefully, he'd patched things up with Mom.

Despite the late hour, I texted Andre.

Joss: Episode 2 went live.

Andre: Already? Must have been a hot one.

Joss: Ace had some interesting recollections about Lens during that last week.

Andre: Anything we should be concerned about?

Joss: Maybe.

Andre: Joss...

Joss: Hey, it's been forever since we've hung out.

Andre: Okay. My place, 7p.m. I'll cook.

Joss: Woo-hoo! Love you!

Andre: Love you too. Try to get some sleep.

Joss: You too.

I slept pretty good. It was a struggle, but I made myself wait to look at the podcast analytics page. By the time I parked across the street from the café, I could no longer wait. I had almost fifteen minutes until I clocked in.

A big grin crossed my face as I saw the amazing number of downloads. The second episode was doing even better than the first. It was a good decision to launch back-to-back episodes. Only problem was I wasn't sure when or if I could publish another episode. I hoped someone else would come forward.

Ace promised me he would share the folder of photos with me from his and Lens's shared Google account today. I quickly checked my email. Disappointment churned when I saw nothing in my inbox from Ace.

I was about to stuff the phone back in my bag when it buzzed with a DM notification. I glimpsed the Instagram profile and grinned. Then I read the message. My mouth fell open as I re-read it again, slowly feeling a sense of panic.

@MayaMacStyle: *You had no right bringing up my father. That's MY family business, and it has NOTHING to do with Lens. This podcast was supposed to help my mother heal, not drag her through more pain.*

I stared at the message, suddenly feeling a pang in my stomach. Did I make a mistake? I wasn't trying to cause Maya or her mother any distress.

@JossMiller: *I'm sorry! I wondered if Lens might have been interested in what happened to your father. You know, like maybe he was seeking answers. It's just a theory.*

The response came back almost immediately.

@MayaMacStyle: *There's no connection between some random robbery in Atlanta and what happened to Lens here in Charleston.*

Random robbery? I frowned at my phone; I wasn't sure how to interpret Maya's response. Lens found their dad murdered in his art studio. And the police never found his killer. I would want to know what happened.

@JossMiller: *I'm exploring all possibilities.*

@MayaMacStyle: *Maybe I shouldn't have trusted you to do this!*

What? Wasn't the whole point of the podcast to explore what could have happened to Lens? It's a true crime podcast. Listeners wanted to hear theories and background information. Besides, I wouldn't even had thought to pursue the angle if Maya hadn't casually dropped that her father had died. She'd been the one to push me into this investigation, posting about it on social media before I even agreed.

I thought back to yesterday when Devante accused Maya of wanting attention. Maybe this wasn't what the beauty influencer had in mind. Lens's tragic death intrigued me, but his sister's determination to control the narrative and direction of my podcast made me weary.

My phone buzzed again.

@MayaMacStyle: *BTW, I'm working on getting Zara to agree to an interview for the next episode. She was the last person to see Lens alive, so her perspective will be crucial. She's nervous about it, but I think I can convince her.*

I growled in frustration and started typing a response, then stopped. No, I needed to think this through carefully. This was my fourth podcast season, and I knew a few things about investigating. The more you kept digging, the more questions came up. Like, how did Maya feel about Zara marrying Devante? Lens's son was Maya's nephew. That had to be awkward at family events. Was Maya really being a so-called friend pushing Zara to be on the podcast?

I definitely wanted to talk to Zara. But according to what Ace told me about the romantic triangle between Lens, Zara, and Devante, putting her on the podcast could turn into a prime time drama fest.

Was that what Maya wanted?

Doubts about Maya's intentions crept into my mind.

Tuesday, June 10 at 7:30 p.m.

I sat on Andre's couch with my laptop open, scanning through the folder Ace shared with me, feeling quite at home. Andre had a typical bachelor pad with an impressive flat screen television taking center stage. His mother and sisters helped him soften the place with earth-tone accent pillows, family photographs, and cozy blankets across his leather seating. Being on the go all-the time, it surprised me that Andre kept his array of plants alive.

Garlic and oregano scents wafted from the kitchen into the living room, making my poor stomach churn with anticipation. My boyfriend loved to cook and his favorite dishes were Italian. I looked up from the laptop screen, my hunger went beyond food. As Andre glided around his kitchen, I admired his athletic build, so often hidden underneath a suit. Tonight, he wore lightweight gray pants with a black muscle shirt. His biceps looked pretty delicious to me. It had been way too long since we'd spent any time together. A few days apart felt like weeks.

Andre caught me staring and flashed a devastating smile before placing a lid over the simmering pasta sauce. "It'll be ready in ten minutes."

I pressed my hands against stomach. "I can't wait. I'm starving."

Andre laughed as he crossed over into the living room and sank down beside me. "This task force has been consuming my life." He nodded toward my laptop. "What do you have there?"

"Not yet. After we eat." I closed the laptop, even though I really wanted to search through the photos, and rested my head against Andre's shoulders. "I've missed this, us."

"Me too." He lifted my chin and kissed me. We lingered there, looking into each other's eyes until Andre shifted his gaze toward the kitchen. "Alright, let me get this off the stove so we can eat."

I trailed behind Andre. With my laptop tucked under my arm, I veered off toward the dining area where I'd done my small part by setting the table. Andre piled a generous amount of spaghetti on each plate. My mouth salivated as I watched him ladle the rich tomato sauce over the noodles. But the true star of this dinner belonged to the golden chicken breast smothered with bubbling parmesan cheese. Out of all the meals Andre fixed, his Chicken Parmigiano was my absolute favorite.

I rubbed my hands together as Andre walked over with both plates, setting one in front of me. I closed my eyes and inhaled the steamy plate of goodness. "I know you had a busy day, but I really appreciate you making this tonight."

Andre grinned. "I figured we needed something other than pizza and Chinese food for a change. Let's bow our heads."

After Andre said grace, we dug in. We ate in silence with only the comforting sounds of our utensils and chewing.

Andre broke the silence by pointing to my laptop. "Are you going to share what you've been sitting on since last night?"

"Not yet." I patted the top of my laptop. "I hope you're in the mood to do some digging."

Andre raised an eyebrow. "Digging? Are you sure we shouldn't turn over whatever you have to Wilkes. I don't need her on my back thinking we're taking over her investigation."

I wiped my mouth with the napkin. "If you find something, you can share it with her. We're doing her a favor, saving her some busy work."

"I'm not sure I like the idea of busy work. It's pretty late." He picked up his empty plate.

"Let me get that. Remember, you do the cooking and I clean." It didn't take me long to load the dishwasher and pack up the rest of the food. I'd purchased some containers so Andre could take his leftovers for lunch the next day.

With the dishwasher running softly in the background, I grabbed my laptop and sat down beside Andre on the couch. He'd turned on the television and appeared to be flipping through ESPN channels.

"You're going to want your undivided attention on this." I pulled up the shared Google Drive folder that Ace had sent me the link to. "This is Lens's backup for his photos. There are dozens of folders organized by date and location."

Andre quickly switched off the television and swiveled his body to look closer at my computer screen. "What? How did you get access?"

I explained to him how Ace and Lens shared a Google account via their YouTube channel. "Apparently, Lens starting using Google Drive. But Ace didn't know until he got a notice about an expired credit card."

Andre moved closer to me, our thighs touching as I clicked through the folders. Not exactly the most romantic activity, but soon we were enamored by Lens's street photography. I recognized some photos from Lens's Instagram.

"These are incredible," Andre murmured. "He really had an eye."

"I know, right?" I clicked on a folder labeled "ATL April" and then noticed the dates for the photos. My fingers tingled with excitement. "Andre, look. These were uploaded a few weeks before Lens died. He must have taken these on his last trip to Atlanta. I wonder if I'm on the right track."

Andre touched my hand. "Right track about what?"

"Oh, didn't I tell you about Lens's dad? He was killed seven years ago in his studio. That's why Lens moved back to Charleston."

Andre tilted his head. "And what were you thinking?"

"If it was my dad, I would still want to know what happened. Ace and I talked about it in the second episode. In fact, Maya DM'd me. She was pretty upset with me for bringing it up."

I was scrolling down the grid of photos when Andre grabbed my hand.

"Wait! Scroll back up."

"Okay, okay." I squinted my eyes, trying to figure out what caught Andre's attention. There was a group of warehouses with several cars parked outside. I wasn't a photography expert, but I wondered if Lens had taken the photos with a zoom lens.

"What am I looking at?"

Andre studied the screen intently. "I've seen that building somewhere else."

"When?" I asked.

Andre leaned back against the couch. "Remember what I told you about Lens possibly being mixed up with dangerous people?"

I hesitated. "Yes."

"Well, maybe he left Atlanta to protect himself. That's what we need to find out." Andre reached for his phone. "I'm calling Detective Wilkes. She needs to see these photos."

I caught his arm. "Wait. Let me look through more of these first. If we're going to bring Wilkes in, I want to have a complete picture of what Lens was doing."

Andre hesitated. "Okay. I guess it wouldn't hurt to tell her in the morning. But, Joss, you can't tell anyone about these, including Ace."

As I clicked through more folders, I wondered why Lens had taken pictures of this warehouse. Had it gotten him killed?

While I knew not to push, my boyfriend seemed to recognize something way out of his jurisdiction. Did these photos have to do with the task force Andre had been assigned to work the last few weeks? He and Nate had been spending time together too. Could it have something to do with my brother's undercover work in Atlanta?

Chapter 13

Simmering Chaos

Wednesday, June 11 at 9:31 a.m.

I woke up on my day off, aware I wasn't in my own bed. I spent the night at Andre's a few nights a week. Not in his bed, though. I didn't know how we managed, but we'd been together for over a year and a half and the most time I'd spent in his bed was to sit on it while talking to him. We both agreed to maintain our celibacy.

Well, Andre insisted I sleep in the guest bedroom.

I tried to tell Leesa and my mom this, but they still didn't believe that Andre and I weren't rolling in the sack like any other healthy young couple. That's probably why I kept getting the 'when are you two getting married' comments a lot more frequently. Even Andre was getting flak from his mom and sisters.

Sometimes I wondered if maybe he was afraid of commitment. But that would be crazy, right? I mean, we were still together. In my bones, I felt like Andre was the one. I didn't want to be wrong about it.

My only competition was Andre's job. He often said that being in a relationship with a homicide detective was not for the faint at heart. Since I produced a podcast about true crime, in my mind, we were a perfect fit.

Both of my best friends, Leesa and my oldest friend, Carmen Patterson, were married. Carmen was trying really hard to become a mom. Once she got pregnant, I would fall even more behind. I think drawing close to thirty was doing something to my brain. I was feeling being husbandless and childless more intensely, as if life was passing me by. But that wasn't true. My great aunts never married or had kids. They both lived good lives.

Andre and I stayed up long past midnight, going through the hundreds of photos in Lens's drive. I'd pulled up his Instagram profile and found a pattern. Lens had structured his folders, separating the photos he'd already posted. I wondered how he chose which photo to share with the public, they all were so good.

My phone buzzed next to me. Then, my phone started blowing up.

I sat up in the bed, alarmed at the sudden influx of notifications.

What is going on?

I grabbed my phone and opened the Instagram app. All the tags seemed to come from a reel of the episode with Ace. I had posted a quick sound bite, not the entire episode.

JOSS: *Anything different about him before his death.*

ACE: *[paused] I noticed something but didn't really pay much attention until after I found out he died. That should have been a happy day, you know? Lens had a way of being the life of any party. He took photos like usual, always had his camera around his neck. But he barely smiled.*

I scrolled to read through the comments. Tre Kennedy had posted the top comment generating the longest thread.

@DaTruthPoetry: *listened to @JossMiller's latest Cold Justice episode. Interesting how Ace mentioned the birthday party. @CavanaughPhotos, remember that day!*

@CavanaughPhotos: *@DaTruthPoetry stop trying to create drama where none existed. This podcast is stirring up pain for people @JossMiller*

@DaTruthPoetry: *@CavanaughPhotos Drama! My man died! Bro was upset for DAYS after that conversation. What did you say to him, D?*

@MayaMacStyle: *@CavanaughPhotos @DaTruthPoetry Wait, WHAT?! Devante, what aren't you telling us?! I didn't know you two had some kind of argument?!*

I placed my hands on the sides of my face. "This is crazy!" Maya had the nerve to go off on me yesterday about stirring up family drama. What did she think she was doing?

Of course I wanted to generate online discussion about Lens, but not like this. I jumped out of the bed. My day off might not be as relaxing as I wanted it to be. After a shower, I gathered my overnight bag and headed to the kitchen. The coffee Andre had brewed was still warm in his thermal coffee pot. I poured a cup and then smiled when I found a note alongside another one of my favorites.

I quickly read Andre's note, thankful for some positivity this morning.

Joss, I hope you enjoy your day off! There's cream cheese in the fridge to go along with those bagels. Talk to you later. Love you!

I held the note to my chest. Our relationship might seem slow to other people, but we had the real deal. I thanked the Lord for answering my prayers for a good man.

I turned the phone's screen away from me so I could enjoy my bagel with cream cheese. While I ignored my phone, my brain kept processing. There wasn't much I could do about the comments online, but it got me thinking back to my discussion with Devante.

He'd said my podcast was stirring up pain for people. Was he referring to his wife? Could that argument between Devante and Lens the weekend before he died been about Zara? Ace said Lens left the house that night after arguing with Zara.

Why did Lens go down to the water that night? From my conversations with Maya and Ace, Lens had not been a fan of being around deep water.

Had he'd gone there to meet someone he knew.

I had a lot of questions.

I pulled my notebook from my bag and drew a circle at the top of the page before adding Lens's name to the center. Then I drew two lines.

I labeled one line, "The Triangle." Lens, Devante and Zara.

The other line I labeled, "Atlanta/Lens's father."

I was sure Andre had shared Lens's Google drive folder with Wilkes by now. What I couldn't gauge from Andre was the significance of Lens taking photos of that Atlanta warehouse. Since there wasn't anything really artistic about the way Lens shot the photos, he must have had some other reason. I wondered if my brother had any info on the warehouse.

My phone pinged. I flipped my phone over to view the incoming text and frowned.

Unknown: U got to help me.

Who was reaching out to me for help?

My body tensed as the three periods toggled on the screen. Whoever was on the other end had more to say.

Unknown: Your podcast has really upset him. He's acting crazy.

Who did I upset this time? Without fail, my podcast ticked off someone.

Joss: Who is this?

Unknown: Zara. We need to talk!

I blew out a breath, feeling a familiar knot of anxiety tighten in my stomach.

Wednesday, June 11 at 11:45 a.m.

I texted Zara back, agreeing to meet at the café at noon. Even though it was my day off, Sugar Creek Café felt like the safest public place to have this conversation. When I walked through the café door, Ace and Kia were hard at work behind the counter. Customers had already created a line.

Fay walked from the back with a pan of cookies. She peered at me with raised eyebrows. "Joss? What are you doing here on your day off?"

I giggled nervously. "What can I say? Sugar Creek Café is like home."

Fay eyed me as she exchanged the fresh pan of cookies inside the pastry counter with an empty pan. "Is something wrong?"

My shoulders sagged. I couldn't hide anything from Fay if I tried. I drew closer to the counter so only Fay could hear me. "I'm meeting someone about the podcast. This seemed like a safe place."

Fay frowned. "Who are you meeting?"

I blew out a breath. "Zara. Zara Cavanaugh."

"Wait. That's Devante's wife, right?"

I nodded. "Do you know her?"

Fay shook her head. "Not that well. Come on in the back."

I went behind the counter and followed Fay toward the kitchen area. She placed the empty pan in the sink and turned around to face me. "Why does Zara want to talk to you?"

"I don't know if you knew this, but Zara and Lens were a couple before he died. They have a son together."

Fay's eyes widened. She stared at me over her glasses. "What? I didn't know that. I don't know why I thought the little boy was Devante's. But now that I think about it, the child is always with Caroline, Lens's mom."

I blew out a breath. "The podcast has stirred up quite a bit of family drama that I really don't understand." I thought for a moment. "Would it be okay if we used the office in the center? It's more private than out here."

"That sounds like a better idea." Fay wiped her hands on her apron. "You know, Joss, you're practically managing that center already. The event planning, the programming, and coordinating with artists. Maybe it's time to make that office officially yours, anyway."

I felt the familiar tug in my chest. Fay had been hinting at this for months. She seemed to be pushing me toward managing the center, but the café was where I felt most at home. It's where I'd learned to connect with people.

"I appreciate that, Fay. But my heart's still inside the café, you know?"

Fay smiled. "I know. But hearts can grow to love new things too."

The café door chimed as I headed from the kitchen back up front. I caught sight of Zara hesitating in the doorway. She glanced over her shoulder as if someone might be following her.

"Zara?" I waved her over. "Thanks for coming."

She nodded, wrapping her arms around herself. "Is there somewhere private we can talk?"

"Absolutely. Would you like to order anything? I can get it for you."

Zara shook her head. "No. I'm fine."

I unlocked the center's doors, and Zara stepped inside. "I'm happy this place exists. It's been a great addition to Sugar Creek."

"I agree," I said, gesturing down the hall. Zara's footsteps clicked on the linoleum as we moved toward the office across from the classrooms.

"Are you into art?" She'd been involved with two photographers, so I assumed there was some interest.

She nodded. "I used to paint."

"Oh, that's cool!" I opened the office door and flicked on the light.

Zara stepped in, and I closed the door behind us.

"Have a seat." Across from the modern wooden desk was a small seating area with two high-back chairs. No one would recognize them as the old worn chairs from the café's back room. Reupholstered in a suede caramel fabric and accented with hunter green throw pillows, the chairs now added to the comfy, earthtone look of the office.

Zara sat on the edge of the seat, placing her hands in her lap.

I sat down across from her. "You said you used to paint. What happened?"

"Life happened." Her eyes flitted around the room. "It's hard to find time to create when you're taking care of a child."

"Oh, yeah. Ace mentioned you and Lens had a son. J.J."

She gave a small smile. "Yes. He's four."

"I hope to meet him someday. Is he at daycare?"

Zara's eyes finally landed on me. "No. Lens's mom takes care of him during the day."

"I can imagine having her grandson around brings her some comfort."

Zara slowly slid back, allowing her back to rest against the chair. "Being around each other helps them both."

I waited to see if Zara would offer the reason we were here. When the silence dragged on a bit too long, I cleared my throat. "Your text said someone was acting crazy. Am I to assume that you were referring to Devante? I saw some of the back and forth on Instagram under the podcast post."

Zara's shoulders sagged. "Since your podcast started, he's been... different. Angry all the time. He threw his phone across the room this morning after reading those comments online."

I leaned forward, studying her face. "Why is he so angry?"

Zara's eyes filled with tears, and she looked away. "I think something is eating away at Devante. Maybe he's guilty about something."

Guilty about what?

"Tell me about how you met Devante."

Zara wiped her eyes with the back of her hand. "Devante and I were together in high school. He got a scholarship to SCAD, and he moved to Savannah. I stayed here and went to the College of Charleston. It was better for me to stay close to home. My mom was sick and needed help."

"That's understandable. So you and Lens?"

Zara sighed deeply. "When I met Lens, I hadn't really dated anyone since Devante. Lens was different. He saw me, really saw me. We started as friends, talking about art and life. Then..." She smiled through her tears. "Then J.J. came along. Lens wanted to get married, but I thought it was okay if we waited a while. I don't know why. Most women would be happy if the man in their life were ready to make that commitment."

"But you weren't ready?"

Something flashed in Zara's eyes. She appeared angry. "I had so much happen to me. My mother passed away from her illness. I was trying to survive. Don't get me wrong, I loved Lens, and I know he loved me. But he could get so wrapped up in his work. Him and his camera. He was living his dream."

"So, while you were with Lens, where was Devante?"

"He was still in Savannah. I think he lived in Atlanta for a while, but eventually, he ended up back here."

"Was there any animosity between him and Lens? I mean, they were cousins. But you and Devante hadn't been together in years."

Zara twisted her fingers in her lap. "There was some awkwardness. Mostly from Devante. At first, Lens didn't know that we'd dated. I think Maya said something to him about it." Zara bit her lip. "Lens was mad about it. I was like I can't help who I dated before you. But Lens was concerned with him and Devante being cousins. Didn't want to cause any drama between his mama and her sister."

"I'm sure you heard the podcast episode with Ace. Do you know what Lens and Devante argued about at J.J.'s birthday party?"

Zara bit her lip. "I don't know. Lens wouldn't talk to me about it. When he was upset about something, he went inside himself."

My phone buzzed with an incoming text. "Sorry, go ahead."

Zara shook her head. "I was saying when Lens was upset, he wouldn't share anything until he was ready."

I had to ask. "Do you think Devante did something to Lens? He's been against covering Lens's death on the podcast from the beginning."

Zara opened her mouth, but no words came out. From the fear in her eyes, I had a feeling she'd been considering that possibility. But did she know anything? Like where was Devante that night?

My phone buzzed again. Then again.

"Zara, I'm sorry, but something's happening." I grabbed my phone to peek at the group of texts flying across my phone's screen.

Fay: Devante walked in asking for you.

Fay: He's acting really strange. Sweating, pacing.

Fay: Joss he looks BAD. I'm calling the police.

I jumped up from the chair and slightly opened the office door.

The office was a good distance from the center's double doors. Even with the lunch hour crowd, the noise level inside the café usually remained subdued, just quiet chatter and the sound of jazz streaming from the ceiling speakers.

But I could hear a man's voice.

Zara came up behind me, her eyes wide with fear. "Oh no! That sounds like Devante."

Was Devante falling apart because he killed his cousin?

Wednesday, June 11 at 12:34 p.m.

"Where is she? I know she's here! Zara! Zara!"

Through the center's double doors, I could make out Devante's side profile. I could also see Fay standing at the counter with her phone pressed up against her ear, probably on the phone with the 911 dispatcher. Behind her, Ace and Kia stood close to each other. Both baristas were eyeing Devante.

I caught sight of Eleanor's wide eyes in her usual booth. I hadn't realized he was here, but Claude sat across from her.

Several people were seated waiting for a quick bite to eat for lunch.

The door chimed and two women walked in laughing, oblivious to what was going on.

"Zara!" Devante shouted.

The two women stopped and reached out to clutch each other. They both turned toward the door, but then three students piled into the café, sending the women back inside. All of them stood frozen in place, not sure if they should run or wait to make their order.

Devante was causing pure chaos during lunch hour. How did he even know to come here looking for Zara? Then, it dawned on me. So many people used location sharing these days. Zara may have led him right to her without knowing.

Next to me, Zara clasped her hands around her face. "I shouldn't have come here. I have to stop him before he does something stupid."

She shoved at the doors.

I grabbed her arm. "Zara, wait—"

Zara wrenched her arm out of my hands. "We have to do something."

I held up my hand. "Fay called the police."

I watched as Zara's face crumbled. "No! No! I was trying to keep the police out of this. He just..."

I stared at her. "He what? Why would you not want the police? He came into a public place and he's..."

Clearly lost his mind!

I peered through the glass doors again to get a better look at Devante. He wore a wrinkled white shirt over jeans, and even from this distance, a sheen of sweat appeared on his face.

Was he on something?

I'd been around people who dabbled in illegal drugs. I wondered if Devante's behavior had been chemically-induced.

Before I could stop her, Zara pushed through the double doors into the café. "Devante! What are you doing here?"

I followed behind her and stood next to Zara, hopefully as a united front if Devante attacked.

He spun around, and I got my first clear look at his face. His pupils were so large they almost swallowed the brown of his irises. His hands shook as he pointed at Zara.

"You think I don't know what you're doing?" His words came out rapid-fire, slightly slurred. "Talking to her, telling her things about me. You trying to make me look bad?"

"Devante, you're scaring people." Zara's voice was calm, but I could see her hands trembling.

In the distance, police sirens blared.

Zara crossed her arms around herself in a hug. "They're going to take you away."

"Why?" He laughed. "I've done nothing."

Fay stated. "You're disturbing my customers. And doing it during lunch hour. I see the police now."

I turned toward the big windows by the booths, as did many others. A police cruiser pulled up in front of the café with flashing lights.

Devante held his arms around his head as if he was trying to keep his head from exploding. He was definitely high on something stimulant-based. This was not the same man who taught camp kids how to work a camera last week.

Suddenly, his head shot up, his wild eyes locked on me. "This is all your fault. You and Maya. Stirring up things."

I thought back to my question only a few minutes ago. Was Devante guilty about something? Was he falling apart now because he was responsible for his cousin's death?

The café door chimed and two police officers entered. One young and tall, the other average height and build but definitely more mature in age than the taller policeman. Both immediately scanned the scene.

"Charleston PD." The younger one said.

I recognized both the officers as regulars at the café.

Fay pointed to Devante. "This man is disturbing my customers."

"I think he's on something." I warned the cops. "Look at him."

Both police officers glanced at me, and then they split away from each other, cautiously approaching Devante.

Devante shook his head, glaring at the two officers. "I haven't done anything," he shouted.

The older cop demanded. "Sir, can you put your hands up so we can see them?"

Zara whimpered. "Do what they say, Devante."

I silently prayed he would go with them. But Devante looked around, skittish like a trapped rat in a corner. I was really worried about what he had taken to make him act this way. Would he do something rash? I hoped not. Sugar Creek Café was a fixture in the community, a haven for students, working professionals, tourists, and many members of the community.

The younger cop stepped forward, his hand on the gun in its holster. "We asked you to raise your hands. We want to keep everyone safe."

Suddenly Devante's stance slumped, almost like he crumbled in on himself. Even his eyes seem to have adjusted as he swung from looking at Zara and me to the cops in front of him. Slowly, he held his hands out in front of him.

The older man barked, "Hold them up higher!"

Devante did as he said. His face appeared blank, his eyes not focused on anyone or anything.

Beside me, Zara openly sniffled as tears streamed down her face. I patted her back, not really sure what else to do.

As the cops handcuffed Devante, I couldn't help but wonder what secrets the man had been hiding. Why was this podcast affecting him this way if he wasn't guilty of something?

Chapter 14

Breaking Point

Wednesday, June 11 at 1:56 p.m.

After the police placed Devante in the back of the cruiser, they pulled a crying Zara outside to talk to her. I wasn't sure how much she was telling them. Not sure what else to do, I typed a message to Maya.

> **JOSS:** Hey, Maya, there was an incident at the café today with Devante. He showed up looking for me. It was really bad! The police arrested him.

> **MAYA:** WHAT?? Are you okay? Where's Zara?

> **JOSS:** I'm fine. Zara is giving a statement to the police now. She's pretty shaken up. Can you come down here?

MAYA: Of course! I'm leaving now. Is she at the café or the police station?

JOSS: Still at the café, but they'll probably take her to the station soon.

MAYA: On my way. This is so messed up.

JOSS: I'm so sorry, Maya. I feel terrible about this whole situation.

MAYA: Not your fault. I knew something was wrong with Devante!

So other people in the family had suspicions about Devante. But when did it start? I'd learned the hard way that killers could be right under your nose. Though it was my day off, I couldn't go back home. I had too many questions. I also felt pretty guilty about what happened.

Ace and Kia moved behind the counter, taking and filling orders as if they were zombies. I figured it wouldn't hurt for me to help my traumatized co-workers, so I pitched in and helped clean up the tables.

Fay came up behind. "You can go back home, you know. It is your day off."

I shook my head. "I shouldn't have met Zara here. That was a terrible idea."

Fay rubbed my shoulder. "You didn't know that was going to happen."

I closed my eyes. "I know, but I still feel awful. Didn't you think he was on something? He wasn't like that last week. It was like two different people."

Fay nodded. "Yes, he was definitely high on some type of substance. That's why I immediately called the police. I feel bad for his mother."

"And Lens's family. I noticed some of your customers took out their phones. This may be on social media by now."

Ace came up behind us, holding out his phone. "It is. Look."

Fay stood on one side and I on the other, peering down at the screen.

A shaky phone video was playing, clearly shot by someone sitting at one of the café tables. The angle showed Devante from the opposite side I'd witnessed.

"Jesus," Fay whispered. "Look at his eyes."

Even on the small phone screen, Devante's dilated pupils were obvious. Whoever was holding the phone camera made a comment. "This is crazy. That guy is totally tweaking."

The video ended as the police led Devante away.

Ace stepped back, placing the phone back in his pants pocket. "Twenty-two shares already. And it was posted ten minutes ago."

I felt sick to my stomach.

This could get really bad. Why did I think coming to the café to meet with Zara was a good idea?

The door chimed, and Fay touched my shoulder. "Uh oh! Looks like this caught the attention of more than people on social media."

I turned around to see what caught Fay's attention.

It was Andre. Just the person I needed at the moment.

But then one of my least favorite people walked in behind him.

Detective Sara Wilkes.

By the look on Andre's face, I might be in trouble.

Wednesday, June 11 at 2:32 p.m.

Thankfully, Detective Wilkes didn't want to talk to me. At least not yet. Instead, she pulled Zara to the side to talk to her. I offered the privacy of the center, which Wilkes gladly accepted.

The detective questioned Zara inside the same office where I'd been talking to the distraught woman. I couldn't imagine what she was going through, and now it was out in the world.

This would affect their marriage. The family. Devante's business.

And this all stemmed from my podcast.

"Are you okay?"

Andre stayed in the café with me, his eyes studying me as if I'd gotten hurt.

"I'm fine. Shocked. Devante should get tested, he was definitely on something. I can't believe that was the same guy who was one of the camp instructors last week." Then I had a horrible thought. "What will the parents think?"

Andre soothed. "It's not your fault, babe. I'm sure they are going to check what he has in his system. Do you know why he showed up here? Did he threaten you?"

"No, I wouldn't say that. The podcast on Lens has gotten under his skin. He's been against it from the beginning." I explained to Andre how Zara had reached out to me for help. "I'm not sure if she thought I could do something. To be honest, it felt more like she was trying to tell me something."

We were sitting in the back of the café. This area was pretty popular with students and bookworms. Fay set up various sitting areas that included comfy chairs across from each other with coffee tables in between. Andre and I had chosen a sitting area in the corner near the windows. It was a beautiful day, and the sun's rays were a comfort. Hard to believe we'd had a crazy man disrupt the usual peaceful vibe of the café.

I must have zoned out. When I came back to myself, Andre was holding both of my hands in his, warming them. He gently massaged my clammy hands and asked, "What do you think she was trying to tell you?"

I thought back to my conversation with Zara. "Before Devante showed up, I asked her if she thought Devante might have done something to Lens."

Andre raised an eyebrow. "And what did she say?"

I shook my head. "She never answered. But she seemed afraid, like maybe she'd considered it. I wonder with her history with him and Lens, if that triangle caused a rift between the two cousins."

Andre kept my hand in his. "People have killed for really minor things. Love and jealousy would be the top reasons."

I nodded, and then my thoughts kicked in. "Why are you and Wilkes here? You're both homicide. Nobody died."

Andre grimaced. "No, we heard down at the station there'd been a call from dispatch to the café. I didn't even realize you were here since it was your day off until I saw the video."

I cringed. "Wow. That video went viral?"

"Yes, it did. Imagine my surprise. There's a man going berserk at my girlfriend's workplace. I'm thinking, Joss is off, she's missing all the action. And then, there you are, smack dab in the middle."

"I wasn't in the middle. I mean..."

Andre leaned in, his concern turned up a notch. "He was not happy with you, and this could have been much worse. Suppose he had a weapon?"

I gulped. I didn't want to think about that.

"You know I try to be careful. Nothing was said on the podcast that was that bad. At least I don't think so. I carefully edited the episodes."

Andre sighed deeply. "Something triggered Devante."

I thought back to the episode. Then I remembered the thread. I pulled out my phone. "You know this all went downhill when Devante was called out on social media. Ace talked about this argument that Devante had with Lens during his son's birthday party." I scrolled to the thread and handed my phone to Andre.

I observed Andre as he read through the comments.

After a few minutes, he handed my phone back to me. "It sounds like this thread is trying to push Devante forward as having a motive to do something to Lens. What's the history between them?"

I shrugged. "They're cousins. And the only thing I've found that could be a conflict is Devante dated Zara in high school. Later, Zara started dating Lens, and they have a son together. After Lens died, Zara and Devante married."

Andre blinked several times as if that would help him process what I'd told him. "That all sounds crazy, but that doesn't mean Devante did anything to his cousin."

"Do you think Wilkes is going to re-open Lens's case? Can she even do that after the coroner ruled he died from drowning?"

"Listening to your podcast has spurred her to take another look. I'm sure she's going to interview Devante after she finishes in there with Zara. If anything, she has someone to look into, track Devante's whereabouts that night."

"It would be good to know what that argument was about. I asked Zara, but she didn't seem to know."

My adrenaline from earlier had faded with Andre's presence. In the distance, I heard the café door chime. I didn't pay it any attention until I heard a voice.

"Where is Zara?" Maya's voice carried across the café.

Even though I was the one who texted her, I suddenly remembered that Maya could be as volatile as her cousin.

Wednesday, June 11 at 3:15 p.m.

I grabbed Andre's hand. He tilted his head, his eyebrows furrowed in concern as he squeezed my hand gently. We couldn't see her, but we could hear her. I took a deep breath and rose from the table. With Andre at my back, we entered the main area of the café. The café usually wasn't full at this time of day. Today, it felt more empty than usual.

Only our regular, Eleanor was still holding down her booth. She sat with her eyes wide behind her glasses. We exchanged a look as Andre and I passed. They say writers get inspiration from real life. Having read some of Eleanor's books, I was pretty sure she'd added to her repertoire of ideas for future books with today's drama.

As we drew closer to the counter, I realized Maya had not come alone. Tre was with her. Since they were a couple, I was glad she had someone to support her. I certainly appreciated Andre being here.

Ace stood behind the counter with a frown on his face. "Maya, Zara is talking to the detective. I guess you've seen the video by now."

Maya rubbed her hands up and down her arms as if she'd caught a chill. "If there wasn't video, I wouldn't have believed it. My cousin has completely lost his mind. Hopefully, they will keep him in jail. I'm gonna make sure Zara gets a restraining order."

I walked up to the counter. "Hey, Maya. Why don't we sit down and talk?"

Maya spun around. "Joss! Thank you for reaching out to me. I knew Devante was against the podcast, but I couldn't for the life of me figure out why." She swung her arms in the air. "I still don't get it."

Tre placed his arm around Maya. "Something's really wrong with bro. We need to protect Zara and little J.J."

I glanced up. Fay had stepped out of her office. I'd brought enough trouble for my boss today. "Hey, why don't we head into the back to wait on Zara?"

Andre added. "It might be awhile before Detective Wilkes finishes interviewing Zara. She may want to talk to you as well."

Maya's eyes narrowed as she followed behind us. "Detective Wilkes?" She sucked her teeth. "Well, it's about time she did her job. It seems to me she should look into what Devante knows about my brother's death."

Tre rubbed Maya's shoulders. "Give the detective some grace. The coroner said Lens accidentally drowned."

"We don't believe that. We never did." Tears formed in Maya's eyes. Instead of heading back to the seating area by the window, I led us all to the area that had a couch and two chairs. Maya eased down on the couch, her hand in Tre's.

She took a deep cleansing breath and wiped her eyes. "I didn't want to think this about family, but I knew something was wrong. The way Devante acted whenever anyone brought up Lens. He tried to discourage me from approaching you about the podcast. From day one! I thought he couldn't possibly still be tart about Zara and Lens's relationship."

I sat in the chair across from the couch and Andre took the other one.

I leaned forward. "Was he jealous? I mean, when Lens was alive."

Maya guffawed. "Absolutely. Devante was the one who left Zara in the dust. Wanted to get his career off the ground by getting his fancy degree. Then, years later, he returns to Charleston as if he could pick up where he left off."

It made little sense why Devante would still be jealous. Lens died two years ago. He and Zara rekindled their relationship and married. The man's behavior was definitely suspicious. I'd already been leaning in the direction Maya was suggesting even before Devante created havoc.

"I feel bad he came to the café. I thought it would be a safe place for Zara and me to talk."

"Don't apologize," Maya cut me off. "I know it looks bad, but that video might be exactly what we needed. Now everyone can see what Devante's really like. I hope they arrest him for Lens's murder."

"Whoa!" Andre held up his hands. "They would need to find evidence first to build a case."

I added. "Yeah, plus Devante doesn't act like that all the time. You saw how good he was with the kids last week. If you really look at him, he wasn't well."

Tre spoke up. "You think he was on drugs?"

Maya gasped. "Drugs? What kind of drugs?"

I turned to Andre, hoping he had an answer.

Andre crossed his arms. "Based on his behavior today, he might have been on a stimulant. I'm sure they will have him take a drug test."

"I had no idea." Maya shook her head. "I mean, I knew something was off about him. But drugs? He could be arrogant, but he's never even been a drinker. That's one thing both Lens and Devante had in common. They weren't into putting stuff in their bodies. The only high they got was being behind the camera."

Tre shifted uncomfortably beside her. "Actually, Maya... I saw Devante take something that looked weird to me."

We all turned to face him. Even though Tre was a large man, he seemed to shrink from the scrutiny.

Andre leaned forward. "Can you describe the pill more specifically?"

Tre rubbed his forehead as if trying to recall. "I barely even take Tylenol, so it caught my attention. It was small, bright blue... I think it had some kind of marking on it. Maybe a symbol? I didn't get a great look. Devante noticed me watching him and popped it in his mouth really quick. Didn't even drink any water."

"Did it look like a lightning bolt?" Andre asked.

Tre's eyes widened slightly. "You know, it might have. Do you know what kind of pill that was?"

Andre gave a quick nod, his jaw hardening. "Sounds like a street drug called Bolt. Synthetic stimulant, highly addictive."

Maya stared at Tre. "Why didn't you say anything? Why didn't you tell me he was using drugs?"

Tre shrugged. "I wasn't sure what I saw. And I try to keep out of people's business. Like I said, I take nothing more than Tylenol if I have to. He could have been taking Aleve or something for a headache. The only reason I remember is because of how he acted when he caught me looking." Tre rubbed his goatee. "Almost like he was ashamed or nervous."

Andre inquired. "Do you remember exactly when this was?"

Tre's eyes flitted from Andre to Maya and then to me. His eyes held mine. "Last week, after he left your camp."

I felt a chill. I let this man around children.

I didn't have time to linger over the anxious thoughts that pummeled me. From where I sat, I had a good view of Wilkes emerging from the center with Zara, who appeared emotionally drained.

I hadn't been interrogated by Wilkes, at least not yet.

When her eyes locked on me, I knew that was probably about to change.

Wednesday, June 11 at 4:06 p.m.

Zara left with Maya and Tre. I felt bad for her and wondered if she knew about her husband dipping into drugs. I wanted to ask Andre more about this Bolt pill, but Wilkes stood in front of me.

This was not my first or even second run-in with Detective Sara Wilkes. While Andre mentioned her every so often, I hadn't seen her in almost two years, since my first podcast. She'd cut her long red hair into a stylish bob that made her look sophisticated.

"Good to see you, Joss," she said. Her green eyes sparkled with questions I was pretty sure she was about to pepper me with. "Can we talk for a minute or two?"

I nodded, wanting to get this over as quickly as possible. "We can go back to the center's office." I glanced over at the counter. Fay wasn't there, and I didn't want to bring any more attention to the café than I had already.

Andre touched my arm. "I'm coming with you."

Wilkes frowned. "Detective Baez. I promise I will have your girlfriend back to you in no time."

Andre chuckled. "We actually have to talk about something related. It's a good idea if I came with you both."

Wilkes blew out a breath and spun around quickly.

I glanced at Andre. He grinned back at me, but I could tell from his eyes that something serious was on his mind. Did it have something to do with the suspected drug that Devante might have taken?

We settled into the office in the same seating area where Zara and I had talked a few hours ago. It seemed so long ago now. I'd spent most of my day off between the center and the café.

Andre grabbed a chair and pulled it next to mine. I could tell Wilkes was not pleased about him being here, but they were colleagues. She had to know I would share our conversation with him.

Wilkes pulled out her notebook and clicked her pen. "Let's start with why you decided to investigate Jerome "Lens" McAbee's death for your podcast."

Knowing it had been her case, I knew I needed to tread carefully with my response. I could sense Andre stiffen next to me. Maybe he hadn't thought about the awkwardness.

I placed my hands on my thighs to steady myself. My nerves had me feeling jittery.

"Maya McAbee, Lens's older sister, approached me after she listened to my previous podcast seasons. I know you investigated her brother's death, but Maya and her family didn't believe he died by accidental drowning. Too many things didn't add up, like his missing camera equipment and his fear of deep water. I have to admit I was intrigued after talking to another friend of Lens."

Wilkes nodded. "Would that be Ace Clark, the young man from your second episode?"

Wilkes had been listening. I guess her reputation was at stake.

"Yes. Ace works here at the café. He told me no one came to talk to him, even though he was good friends with Lens. Lens was like his mentor too."

Wilkes scribbled in her notebook as I talked. "Is Ace here today?"

I hesitated for a moment, not wanting to bring any attention to Ace, but Wilkes might find something valuable in talking to him now. "Yes, he's the tall young man behind the counter."

She looked up from her notebook. "When did Zara first contact you about her suspicions regarding her husband? Are you friends?"

I shook my head. "No. I met her last week. She came with Maya to Friday Night Jam. I didn't even know she and Devante were married until recently. I recruited him to help with the media camp last week. He was great with the kids."

I swallowed and looked over at Andre. He gave me an encouraging smile.

I took a breath. "He was a completely different person today than last week. Earlier this morning, I could see a thread on social media where people were asking him about something Ace said in the latest episode. While I was reading the comments, Zara reached out to me."

Wilkes asked. "Can I see the messages?"

I pulled up the post on my Instagram. "I can share the link to this post. And I can screenshot the messages from Zara if it will help."

Wilkes glanced at Andre. "Sure, you can send them to Detective Baez's phone. Baez, can you share them with me?"

"Absolutely." Andre replied.

While I worked to share the information, Wilkes continued to write in her notebook. I heard a ping from her direction. She retrieved the phone clipped to her belt and looked down at what Andre had forwarded to her.

Finally, she asked, "What specifically did you and Zara talk about? Did she mention anything about what happened between Devante and Jerome during this birthday party?"

"She said at the time, Lens... I mean Jerome, shut down about it. She didn't know what the argument was about. I will say Devante was opposed to the podcast featuring Lens's story from the beginning."

Wilkes leaned forward. "What do you mean by opposed?"

"He seemed uncomfortable whenever it came up. Devante thought Maya wanted attention and that we should leave it alone."

"Sounds like he was trying to hide something." Wilkes commented.

It certainly looked that way!

"Will you be testing Devante for drugs? His behavior today was so erratic. I'm feeling really bad that I had him come out and do the photography workshop with the children."

Andre touched my hand. "You can't beat yourself up about that."

I treasured the warmth of his hand on my mine.

He didn't remove it even as he focused on his colleague. "Wilkes, that's what I needed to discuss with you. Based on his symptoms and gathering some info, Devante was likely on a drug we call Bolt on the street. You know the task force has been tracking its distribution here in Charleston."

I turned to stare at Andre. "Wait! That's what the task force is about?"

Andre gave me a quick nod. "We've had seventeen overdoses in the past few years from these blue pills with lightning bolt symbols. Three were fatalities. There's something mixed in this pill that is dangerous. We've been trying to track the source of distribution." His eyes flitted between Wilkes and me. "This could be the break we need if Devante is willing to tell us where he got the pills. That's if he took them."

Wilkes straightened in the seat, her eyebrows furrowed. "I'm sure we'll test for whatever substance he had taken. Are you thinking Jerome's death is connected to this drug operation? It's been two years."

Andre crossed his arms, giving me a look.

I knew that warning. This was confidential information.

Andre explained. "The first two overdoses were right before Lens's death. The doctors weren't sure what caused the overdose. It's my understanding that Lens was considered a street photographer. I looked at some photos he took on his Instagram feed. He didn't select the prettiest people, but those who were down and out. I'm wondering if he ran across something of interest that got him in trouble. That would be motive for murder."

That's when I recalled the photo that had captured Andre's attention from Lens's cloud storage. "The warehouse. Does this have something to do with those pictures on Lens's Google Drive?"

Wilkes asked sharply. "How do you know about those?"

I frowned. "Because I was the one to get access."

Beside me, Andre fidgeted, purposely not looking at me.

Oops, maybe I shouldn't have revealed that.

After all, I was the one who wanted to look through the photos when Andre wanted to give Wilkes access right away.

Wilkes sighed. "Are you planning on publishing any more episodes?"

"I'm not sure." The next person I'd wanted to interview was Zara, but I was certain today's events with her husband had traumatized her.

Wilkes snapped her notebook shut with a sharp crack that made me flinch. "Please keep us in the loop." She stood, glanced over at Andre and then turned her green eyes on me. "And Joss? I'm sure I don't need to remind you to tread carefully."

I gulped, sneaking a glance at Andre. I hoped I hadn't gotten him into any trouble. Now that I knew about the task force connection, I had so many more questions.

Chapter 15

Bitter Aftertaste

Thursday, June 12 at 5:02 p.m.

After yesterday's events, the normalcy of Thursday had me on edge. But it was good to be back behind the counter. If anything, yesterday had brought a steady flow of regular and curious patrons, including several reporters trying to get statements. Last night, Andre told me that Devante would be in the county jail until his bail hearing, which would probably be on Friday. The charges against him included disorderly conduct and drug possession for now.

I imagined that sometime today, they would get a search warrant for the Cavanaugh's home and car. Learning that there were some overdoses and fatalities, Devante was lucky he wasn't one of them. He was a talented photographer, but this could affect his business. I prayed he could recover and that his marriage wouldn't be destroyed.

Of course, I had other issues of my own to deal with. Since being back at work, I had avoided the elephant in the café most of the day. Now that it was less than an hour until closing, I started my usual regime of stocking the back counter with cups. After Ace left at three o'clock, it was me and Fay.

Ace had been excited about finally getting to talk to Wilkes. I'd never known anyone thrilled about talking to law enforcement. Whatever he said to her, Wilkes was working to convince their chief to re-open Lens's case now that some other theories were emerging. At least something good was happening.

I could hear Fay in the back cleaning up pans, getting them prepped for tomorrow. My boss had been quieter than usual today, and that concerned me. I knew yesterday had been hard on her, but she'd done the right thing calling the cops. Devante could have escalated. Fay's priorities had to be protecting her patrons and employees.

I wondered if I'd brought trouble to the café.

I finished stocking the cups and took the plastic that was wrapped around them to the back. After throwing away the plastic, I called out. "Fay?"

"Yeah?" her voice echoed in the kitchen.

"Can we talk for a minute?"

She turned around, her gold oval-shaped glasses clinging to the end of her nose. The frames she sported today gave her a serious professor look. She grabbed a towel and dried her hands. "What's on your mind?"

I crossed my arms over my chest as if to shield myself from any wrath. "I'm really sorry about yesterday. I know having police here and all that drama... it's not good for business." I tried to catch my breath. "And you're mad at me, right?"

Fay pushed her glasses up her nose and walked over to me. "Joss, honey, you did the right thing investigating that boy's death. I meant to tell you when I was at bible study last night, Caroline expressed how she really appreciated the attention being brought back to her son. She asked everyone to keep praying."

I blew out a breath, my eyes stinging from sudden tears. "Really? I keep wondering if this family is going to suffer more. Devante was out of his mind yesterday, threatening his wife in public. I'm scared about what else is going to happen."

Fay placed her hands on both of my shoulders. She was a tall woman, so I had to look up at her. Her eyes were warm and sisterly.

"You care about the people you choose to feature on your podcast. It's not about sensationalizing people's pain but helping bring attention and possibly closure. You can't blame yourself for other people's choices. Devante is the one on that video that's circulating."

"But if I hadn't started the podcast—"

"No, Joss!" Fay stepped back and adjusted her glasses. "I could tell something was wrong with Devante the moment he walked in. I've seen people on drugs before. That wasn't your doing. The entire world saw that Devante had something going on with him."

My shoulders sagged. "Are you sure you're not mad at me?"

"Of course I'm not mad at you." Fay shook her head. "Give yourself some grace, okay?"

I blew out a breath, feeling some tension leave my body.

Fay crossed her arms. "You know who I do feel bad for is Devante's mother. Cassandra is a vibrant, loving woman. She usually is the first one at bible study, leading the lesson. Last night she wasn't there. I'm sure she's devastated. But I found it interesting that her sister showed up. Caroline's attendance at bible study has been sporadic since Lens's death."

I raised my eyebrows. "That is interesting. Seems like the whole family is going through some things."

Fay nodded. "Right! Both those sisters are dealing with their sons now. Caroline's still grieving Lens, and now Devante's mother might have to deal with her son being a substance abuser. I feel for both women."

"I hadn't thought about that," I said.

"Yes. And me and you both know family drama always runs deeper than people realize. So, please. Stop beating yourself up. Besides," Fay winked her eye, "business was good today."

I laughed. "This is true."

The familiar door chime alerted me to a customer. I glanced at the wall clock, we had less than thirty minutes until closing time. "Looks like we have a customer. Let me grab their order."

I sprinted up to the counter and froze mid-step.

Maya.

Thursday, June 12 at 5:31 p.m.

I struggled with keeping the smile on my face. From recent days, I suspected Maya didn't show up at the café pining for a latte or a matcha. Dressed in a pink sundress with strappy sandals that showed off her French-manicured toes, Maya looked like she was going out on the town for the evening. Her hair hung down in a long ponytail that swung as she walked.

"Hello, Maya. You look glamorous!"

She smiled, showing off white teeth framed by ruby red lipstick. "Thank you. I'm on my way to an influencer's event at the Charleston Place Hotel, but I wanted to drop by. How are you doing, Joss?"

I shrugged. "I'm good. Just working here at the café as usual."

"I see. Well, I was hoping we could talk about the podcast when you had a moment."

My smile faltered.

Of course, that's what she wanted.

Behind me, I heard a noise. I turned to see Fay in the doorway carrying a box of creamers. She smiled at Maya and headed over to the condiment area.

If Maya was going to harass me about my podcast, she could at least order something. "What can I get for you?"

Maya frowned as if she didn't really want anything. She looked up at the menu board. "Sure. How about a vanilla latte?"

"Coming right up."

I turned to the espresso machine, grateful for something to focus on besides Maya. The familiar routine of steaming milk and pulling shots usually calmed me, but I could feel Maya watching my every move. I poured the steamed milk into

Maya's cup, creating a small heart design. It was my signature design and the one I was great at. Ace and the younger baristas could pour all kinds of designs. I turned from the machine and placed the cup on the counter before ringing up her order.

"Oooh, that's pretty!" Maya reached into her pale pink clutch.

I thought she was going to take a picture for Instagram. Instead, she tapped her phone against the card reader and announced. "I was thinking about the next episode."

My eyes fluttered up to her face and then back to the register. I knew I must have looked as frustrated as I felt. "Maya, I need time to process everything that's happened."

She whined, "But people are talking, Joss. We need to keep pushing, especially since Devante is still behind bars."

I caught Fay eyeing me as she paused from restocking the creamers.

I licked my lips. "Maya, what exactly are you asking for?"

"Zara needs to be on the podcast. She has the most intimate perspective on what Lens was going through before he died. And now with Devante's arrest..." Maya leaned forward against the counter. "She's the key to everything."

I tried to keep my voice level. "Maya, Zara just went through a traumatic experience." I held up a finger, "One, the police arrested her husband in front of her and there's evidence of his breakdown on the Internet," and then another. "Two, said evidence of his crazy behavior suggests her husband could be abusing drugs." I unfurled my thumb, adding it to the two fingers I was holding up. "And three, the police have questioned her. There is even suspicion about Devante knowing something about what happened to his cousin."

"Exactly! That's why she needs to talk, while it's fresh."

Fay appeared beside me, appearing to wipe down the counter, but I knew she was positioning herself as backup if this conversation went south.

"The woman has a young son, your nephew, to think about. You're her friend. Don't you think she needs time to process, not to be put on a podcast that's already caused her life to implode?"

Maya huffed. "You can't stop now when we're getting close to the truth. You only have two episodes out there."

I felt my face growing warm, which meant it was glowing red. "Maya," I said carefully, "Devante is your family."

Maya shook her head. "That doesn't change what he might have done to my brother."

"Isn't this family drama though? I mean, you got upset when I brought up your father's death. You said it wasn't relevant to the podcast. But now you want me to drag your cousin's wife into this mess?"

Maya's eyes flashed with anger. "That's completely different. My father had nothing to do with this. It's about Lens. Justice for my brother. Why can't you—" She stopped mid-sentence, glancing over at Fay, who was openly watching our conversation now. My boss's glasses had slid down her nose and she peered over them glaring at Maya.

Taking a deep breath, Maya forced her smile back into place. "I'm sorry. Just... think about it, okay? Zara's story could help other people in similar situations."

She picked up her latte and headed for the door without another word.

As soon as Maya left, Fay walked over to the door and locked it. It wasn't quite six o'clock yet, but Fay was the boss.

She pointed at me as she crossed the floor. "Joss, you need to watch out for that one."

"What do you mean?"

Fay threw her arms in the air. "Think about it. Who's really benefiting from all this drama? Your podcast is putting the spotlight on her brother's death, but it's also bringing a lot of attention to Maya. Have you checked how much her social media following has grown since this started?"

I felt a chill run down my spine. "No, I hadn't thought to look."

Fay continued. "Sometimes people can love the spotlight a little too much, even when it comes from tragedy."

I recalled what Devante had said to me earlier this week after Maya's episode went live.

Maya didn't even like her brother. They never got along.

Was Maya's intentions really sincere?

Friday, June 13 at 7:30 p.m.

Spending Friday night with friends felt like exactly what I needed. Since there wasn't a Friday Night Jam this week, Andre had invited Chris, Leesa, and Nate over for dinner. The guys were out back grilling steaks while Leesa and I made a big bowl of salad.

"Kisha is still talking about the camp," Leesa said, slicing tomatoes. "She wants to know if you're doing another one this summer."

I put shredded cheese in a serving bowl. "Maybe next year. This week has been... a lot. I still can't believe I let Devante work with those kids when he was using drugs. He seemed really normal, and the kids enjoyed him."

Leesa stopped slicing and looked at me. "Joss, you need to stop beating yourself up about this. You had no way of knowing. Are you finished with this season of your podcast? I heard Wilkes got Lens's case reopened."

I rolled my eyes. "I don't know. Maya has been sending me messages. She seems to think Zara wants to talk, but I haven't heard directly from Zara."

Leesa frowned. "You know I follow Maya online. I had no clue she was Lens's sister, who I also followed. They never crossed over or really showed their family on their feed like some people do. Most people are complaining about her posts."

"Really? Why?"

"Well, you know she's a beauty influencer. People are used to her posting about skincare, makeup and hair products. These past few weeks, every day has been a post about her brother. Here, let me show you her latest post. I thought it was weird." Leesa pulled out her phone, and I slid over to look at the screen.

@MayaMacStyle: Two years without my brother... Lighting this candle at the pier where we lost him. The sunset lighting here is actually incredible for content. Anyway, don't forget to stream my podcast interview! Link in bio! #RIP #SunsetVibes #ContentCreator #JusticeForLens

I studied the photo. Her makeup was perfect and her skin glowed. "She must have taken this selfie yesterday. She was wearing this same outfit when she stopped by the café. She sure doesn't look like she's grieving."

Leesa nodded. "That's what I said. If you read through the comments, other people are saying the same thing. It's complete overkill, like she's milking the sympathy."

Thinking about what Fay said yesterday, I had looked at Maya's account last night. She'd created a reel on Wednesday. It must have been in the morning since she didn't mention Devante at all, but she'd boasted about getting over a million views on her post about Lens. She gushed and welcomed the followers who joined her account this week.

"Did you see this?" Leesa clicked play on the reel.

@MayaMacStyle: Thank you so much for all the love. I appreciate the over two thousand followers I received this week.

I shook my head. "Yes. I saw that post last night. I see what you're saying. It's like she's enjoying the attention too much."

The back door opened, and the three men trickled in carrying platters of perfectly grilled steaks and colorful bell peppers, zucchini, and asparagus. The savory aroma filled the kitchen.

"What are you guys looking at?" Andre asked, setting down the platter of glistening steaks.

"Looking at Maya's account. Oh yeah, and Leesa told me to stop beating myself up."

Nate frowned. "About what?"

I hadn't been in touch with my brother most of the week. "Devante Cavanaugh's meltdown in the café. I'm sure you've seen it on the Internet. He was there a week ago. I'd recruited him to teach the kids a photography session. They loved him!"

Chris commented. "Yea, Kisha thoroughly enjoyed his class. The guy lost it on Wednesday. But last week, he was on his game, perfectly normal. It happens, especially if you choose to dabble in drugs. You can't predict the outcome."

I poured ice tea into the glasses, while everyone fixed their plate. Once we'd settled around the table, Andre led grace. Then we all dived in, chomping on salad and grilled vegetables, knives slicing the tender steak.

Andre commented. "Despite what happened on Wednesday, at least Wilkes was able to reopen Lens's case. That's got to feel good."

I grinned at him. "It does. And this steak is delicious."

Everyone around the table murmured their agreement in between chewing.

Andre cut into his steak. "Speaking of which, we got the toxicology results back on Devante today. He tested positive for Bolt."

Leesa frowned. "I've never heard of that."

Chris nodded. "It's a small blue pill with a lightning bolt on it. Highly addictive, makes users paranoid and aggressive."

"That explains Devante's behavior."

Andre took a swig of ice tea before responding. "Yeah, he was lucky, though. We've had overdoses and some fatalities."

Leesa asked. "Is this new? Where does it come from?"

Andre answered, "It's been big in Atlanta for a few years. About two years ago, the drug started trickling into Charleston. We didn't really know what it was until this year."

I felt pieces clicking together. "Atlanta." I faced Nate, ready to ask if it was what he'd been investigating, then caught myself glancing at Leesa.

Nate seemed to pick up on my hesitation. "It's okay, sis. They can know." He looked around the table. "I was working undercover in Atlanta investigating a drug trafficking operation. Bolt was one of their main products."

Leesa's eyes widened. "Undercover? Like, for real?"

"DEA," Nate confirmed. "And I hate these drugs made it to Charleston. We've been trying to shut down the distribution network."

"Is there a connection here?" I asked. "Between what you were investigating and what happened to Lens?"

"There's definitely someone with the means to transport drugs from Atlanta to South Carolina," Nate said carefully. "The operation I was tracking had connections throughout the Southeast."

Chris leaned forward. "What's happening with Devante now? Can you find out who his dealer is?"

Andre shook his head. "He made bail this morning. His mother put up her house. We found Bolt pills during the search of his home, but he's not talking about where he got them."

"Why won't he talk? Wouldn't he be able to get a deal with the D.A. if he shared information about the dealer?"

Andre and Nate exchanged a look, both grinning.

Andre smiled at me. "See what I told you? Your sister is totally into law enforcement stuff."

I laughed. "I get it from our dad. Except, I didn't pursue the field like my brother."

We continued eating, but my mind was working overtime. I had so much going on that I couldn't keep it to myself.

"You know Lens was from Atlanta. He went back a few weeks before he died. Everyone I talked to so far said something was different about him when he came back from that trip. If Bolt was here before he died, I wonder what he knew."

Then I thought about something else.

My brother was next to me, and I grabbed his arm, startling him.

"Maya and Tre. You saw them both in Atlanta."

My brother locked eyes with me, understanding dawning.

Friday, June 13 at 11:47 p.m.

I couldn't sleep. And it wasn't because I wasn't in my bed. Inside Andre's guest bedroom, I laid on the bed wide awake. My thoughts swirled around Maya and Tre. Maya had been pushing for what seemed like getting justice for her brother. But her excessive need to play this all out on social media concerned me. And she wanted to involve Zara, whose marriage to the troubled Devante collided with her grief over losing Lens, her child's father. It was all too much.

I cut on the light and pulled out my phone. I hadn't opened Lens's Instagram since last week. Sometimes content creators included the location on their posts. This time, I scrolled through his posts, paying particular attention to the photos that would have been taken in Atlanta. I scrolled and scrolled, finding myself drawn to Lens's artistry.

My eyes were growing heavy. I'd scrolled far enough to notice Lens's earlier posts were different, but that wasn't unusual.

I wasn't sure what to post when I signed up for Instagram. Sometimes I posted selfies, other times I posted new clothes or a new hairstyle. I had a phase where I posted my food, so obsessed with getting the perfect shot even before I ate. My feed still looked chaotic and not carefully curated like popular content creators.

Lens's feed comprised his one-man crusade with his camera, capturing people from all walks of life through photos and sometimes reels. But these few posts revealed another side to Lens. He was a true artist and could draw. There were several carousels of comic book style illustrations of superheroes he'd created. Some resembled superheroes I'd seen before, but others were completely original to my eye.

One character caught my attention making me sit straight up, completely forgetting that a few minutes before I'd grown sleepy.

It was a hero with a lightning bolt emblazoned across his chest.

@BehindtheLensATL: My first original character. Still my favorite symbol.

I stared at the screen, my pulse quickening.

That symbol.

I scrambled out of bed, grabbing my phone. The hardwood floor was cold against my bare feet as I padded down the hallway to Andre's bedroom. I knocked softly at first, then harder when there was no response.

"Andre? Andre, wake up."

Andre snatched the door open. "Joss? What's wrong? Are you okay?"

For a second, I got distracted.

He was wearing pajama pants and no shirt.

Focus, Joss!

I shoved my phone toward him. "Look at this. Does this look like the bolt on that pill?"

He rubbed his eyes and took my phone. I followed him back inside the forbidden zone and sat on his bed as he studied

Lens's drawing. Suddenly, he appeared alert. "Where did you find this?"

"Lens's Instagram. He was an artist too. Looks like he drew it years ago. But what does it mean?" I was speaking too fast, my words tumbling out.

Andre reached for his own phone on the nightstand. He pulled up something, comparing it to my screen. He looked up at me, fully awake now. "I mean there's definitely some similarity."

He turned his phone toward me, displaying the infamous blue pill.

"Do you think Lens had something to do with this, or did someone swipe his design?"

Andre sat on the edge of the bed. "If Lens saw Bolt pills in Charleston or Atlanta, he would have recognized his own design immediately. Maybe that's what was bothering him those last few weeks."

"He would have started asking questions. Trying to find out who was using his art." My mind raced ahead. "Andre, what if his father saw the same thing seven years ago? What if Lance discovered someone using his son's design for something illegal? And they killed him for it."

Andre rubbed my shoulders. "Look, we both need to get some more sleep. I will touch base with Wilkes in the morning. This was a good find, Joss. We need to know everyone who was close enough to Lens to know about his drawings."

I eased my way off the bed with the intentions of heading back to the guest bedroom. Andre grabbed my hand. "Don't go. Stay in here tonight."

I looked into his eyes and smiled. He didn't have to ask me twice.

We both crawled under his covers. Andre held me and I felt the rise and fall of his chest against my back. One of these days, we would make this more official.

My eyes grew heavy despite my racing thoughts. Maya asked me to interview Zara.

But I also had another person in mind.

Chapter 16

Connecting the Dots

Saturday, June 14 at 7:30 p.m.

Settled on Andre's couch, I opened my laptop for the Zoom call. The waiting room notification popped up, and I admitted my guest. The screen flickered to life, and Zara's wary eyes widened when she saw me. I noticed the background appeared familiar.

"Hey, Zara. Are you at Maya's place?"

Zara blinked. "Yes, I'm staying with Maya for now."

For now, while her husband was out of jail. I couldn't blame her. She had a child to protect.

Last night, I sent a text to Zara to see if we could talk. It was late, but she called me to confirm she really did want to be on the podcast. I asked her repeatedly if she was sure. I didn't want my podcast being associated with breaking up a marriage. Of course, her husband had been the main one against me digging into Lens's death. Was he hiding something?

I found it interesting that as much trouble as Devante was in already, he wasn't willing to be a snitch. It made me wonder if his dealer was someone he knew or someone dangerous. A person selling a pill that had already caused fatalities was a person I wasn't sure I wanted to ever meet.

In the background, on the Zoom call, I could hear the voice of a young boy. "Mama."

Zara turned. "Not now J.J. Go with your auntie."

J.J. wasn't haven't it and ran into view of the camera. The young boy stared at me, immediately captivating me.

"Hey, cutie!" I waved at him from my screen.

He grinned, waving back at me. "You're inside the computer."

I laughed. "No, you're inside my computer."

That set him giggling. Zara smiled and kissed her son on top of the head. "Remember I said Mama needs to be on the computer for a while. You need to go with Auntie Maya."

"Okay." J.J. scrunched up his face, then he stared at me, his eyes wide. His big crocodile tears made me want to cry along with him. I stared back at the little one, thinking about pictures I'd seen of Lens. Here was his mini-me.

I'd lost my father too, but I was twenty years old. I had a lifetime of knowing my dad. J.J. was so young. Would he even remember his dad?

J.J. waved at me. "Bye-bye."

I returned his wave, trying to smile as the thought clung to me.

In the background, I could hear Maya but couldn't see her. "Sorry, Zara. He's so fast. He got away from me." Maya poked her head in the frame, making Zara slide over. "Joss, Tre showed up."

Tre was there. Good. Hopefully, I could knock out two episodes.

"Great! Is he willing to talk? Since he and Lens grew up together in Atlanta, I was hoping we could record Tre reciting the poem he wrote."

Maya's eyes lit up. "That's a great idea." She winked. "Don't worry. I will convince him."

I didn't doubt it!

Then it was Zara and me.

"I need to ask again. Are you sure you really want to do this?"

Zara's eyes flickered to something above her, then she focused on me. I could tell from the bags under her eyes, she hadn't been sleeping. Unlike Maya, who had on a face full of makeup, Zara's face was free of makeup with a few blemishes across her cheeks. She was naturally beautiful.

"Yes. I want to talk about Lens. I want people to know how much I love and miss him. And I believe something happened to him that night. I'm pretty sure he was going to see someone."

Was that someone Lens knew?

Was it his cousin Devante? They'd had some beef between them centered around Zara. But my suspicions were starting to lean toward his sister. And his friend, Tre.

COLD JUSTICE PODCAST

Season 4, Episode 3
Behind the Lens - The Wife

Scheduled to Publish on Monday, June 16

JOSS: Welcome back to the *Cold Justice Podcast.* I'm Joss Miller. Since our last episode, there have been significant developments in this case. The Charleston Police Department has officially reopened Lens's case as a homicide investigation. Also, we've come up on the second anniversary of his death. Some of you may have seen his sister, Maya, post about it online.

Today, I'm speaking with Zara Cavanaugh, Lens's girlfriend at the time of his death and the mother of their son.

Zara, thank you for joining me. I know this has been an incredibly difficult time.

ZARA: Thank you, Joss. I needed to do this, especially for our son.

JOSS: Let's start at the beginning. How did you and Lens meet?

ZARA: Lens and I met at an event here in Charleston about five years ago. He was photographing kids at a back-to-school festival. He had this big, beautiful camera hanging around his neck. Lens had a way of making everyone feel comfortable. He snapped some photos of me and then shared them with me. I loved the way he captured me. I'd never seen myself like that before.

JOSS: Your relationship became serious pretty quickly.

ZARA: It did. Lens was... he was everything I'd been looking for. Kind, passionate about his work, great with kids. When I got pregnant with our son, he was so excited. He was there in the hospital room when our son was born. Lens really enjoyed being a father.

JOSS: Let's talk about Lens in those final weeks before his death. He went to Atlanta a few weeks before his death. From the previous podcast, we know he was different after that trip and then also after he had an argument with Devante. Do you know what could have affected him?

ZARA: [Long pause] He was different. Stressed, but also angry in a way I'd never seen before. I know he went to Atlanta to visit his dad's grave. He did that every year. I wasn't able to go with him because our son got sick. We both decided it was best for me to stay home with him.

JOSS: So, he could've been thinking about his father's death. Lance McAbee's death remains unsolved.

ZARA: That sounds about right. Lens would go inside himself when he was upset about something. It's like he had to process it. But I felt like there was something else. I wish he'd told me what was wrong. [Voice breaking] The night he died, we argued. I wanted to know what he was keeping from me. He told me he couldn't tell me yet, but he would tell me soon.

JOSS: That was the last time you saw him. Did he have his backpack with him?

ZARA: Yes, it was the last time I saw him alive. He carried his backpack everywhere so he would be ready to take a photo when he came across something. I asked him where he needed to go. He said he had to do something.

JOSS: Sounds like it was unusual for him to leave the house at that time of night.

ZARA: It was! Lens liked to be in the street taking photos, but he loved being at home at night to relax and process his work. Since J.J. was born, Lens stayed in the house. His schedule was a lot more flexible than mine. People don't know this, but he made a lot of money from his photos and videos online. Companies like Synaptic sponsored him to feature their software. It was good money.

JOSS: That's good to know. Who do you think he went to meet? Would it be someone he knew?

ZARA: [long pause] Yes, only a friend or family member would have gotten him out of the house at night.

JOSS: Zara, I have to ask about the difficult situation you've been in since Lens's death. You married his cousin Devante.

ZARA: [Deep breath] Yes. Devante and I dated in high school before he went to college. After Lens died, he reached out to offer support. I was a single mother, grieving, struggling financially. Devante was there for me, as a friend at first.

Then, I fell for the guy I used to love in high school. This version of him was much older, more mature. And he reminded me of Lens. Always taking photos, except Devante does more commercial photography. He creates these fairytale photos of people getting married.

Lens and I never married. I wanted our son to have a father in the house, and I wanted to be a wife.

JOSS: But things changed. By now, many people have seen the video online. The police have arrested Devante on drug charges and disorderly conduct. How are you processing all of this?

ZARA: I'm relieved my son is safe, but I'm also terrified. I don't want people to think I don't love my husband. I do. I want him to get help and rid himself of whatever demons are plaguing him.

JOSS: Did you know Devante was taking drugs?

ZARA: No, I didn't. Devante has always been such a mellow guy. Sometimes he would get so angry. And a few times, his anger scared my son.

JOSS: When did these angry episodes start? Was this recent behavior or something you noticed earlier in your marriage?

ZARA: [thinking] A few months ago. Lens's mother started talking about Lens. She's been begging the police to look into his death. She would go to the station around his birthday in April, and then again in June, around the anniversary of his death.

JOSS: Oh, so this is fairly recent? Do you think the conversations about Lens's death triggered Devante's drug use?

ZARA: Even before Devante showed up at Sugar Creek Café in that state, I realized my son and I weren't safe. His angry episodes have been increasing, and he stopped going to church with us. I asked him where he was the night Lens died.

JOSS: And what did he say?

ZARA: [sharp breath] He wouldn't answer me. It was a simple question, but he refused to respond. He started throwing things and yelling that I didn't love him. Which isn't true. I do love him.

JOSS: Can I ask why you asked him that? Something must have made you suspect him.

ZARA: It sounds horrible, but he asked me to take down the photos of Lens. He wanted my son to think of him as his father. It felt like he was trying to erase Lens. Devante even wanted me to back off on my son spending time with his Lens's mother. I really asked him the question out of anger. It seemed strange to be so threatened by someone who was gone.

JOSS: Zara, thank you for your courage in speaking out. I really hope Devante gets what he needs and that your family can truly heal and find closure.

ZARA: Thank you for not giving up on Lens's story. If it wasn't for your podcast, we wouldn't have the police investigating his death.

JOSS: Listeners, as this case moves through the official investigation, we'll keep you updated on any developments. If you have any information, please contact Detective Sara Wilkes at the Charleston Police Department.

I'm Joss Miller, and this has been the *Cold Justice Podcast*.

Chapter 17

Grounds for Panic

Saturday, June 14 at 8:45 p.m.

I made sure my camera and audio were off before I looked at Andre and Nate. Both of them had been in the living room while I conducted my interview with Zara. "Did you get anything from listening to Zara? It was a great interview, and I can probably post as is without too much editing."

Andre spoke up. "I thought it was interesting that she thought Lens was going to meet a relative or friend. That seemed pretty specific."

Nate nodded. "She was being cautious about naming anyone directly."

I sighed. "I kind of feel bad about publishing it. But it might force Devante to talk."

Andre leaned back in his chair. "About Tre..."

My stomach tightened. "What do you think Tre knows?"

Nate answered. "When I went to Friday Night Jam last week, I recognized Tre from Atlanta. I've seen him talking to people from my investigation. Could be nothing, but Atlanta's not that small, so his presence raised some red flags for me."

I thought my brother was jealous of seeing Maya with Tre, but he'd seen him before. Then what Nate said clicked in my mind. "Wait, you think Tre might be involved in the drug operation?"

"I don't know," Nate said. "But he travels back and forth from Atlanta to Charleston pretty regularly."

Andre added. "While he wasn't overly specific about the blue pill he claimed he saw Devante taking, he did seem to know enough detail to warrant suspicion. Like could he really have seen the emblem on it? Maybe he knew what that pill looked like up close."

"He's been a smooth operator this whole time. Maya is smitten with him, that's for sure."

Nate huffed. "Which means she listens to whatever he tells her."

Andre added, "Just conduct the interview normally. Ask about his friendship with Lens, about Atlanta, about that trip. Keep it in line with what you've talked about with the other guests. If you feel you have some other questions, go with your instincts. You're good at this, Joss. Do your thing."

My hands felt cold. "What if he gets suspicious?"

"He won't," Andre encouraged. "You're a podcaster and you've done your research. There's no reason for him to suspect anything."

I glanced down at my screen and saw that Maya was on. "You guys hold a minute." I turned on my camera and mic. "Hey, Maya. Is Tre going to let me interview him?"

"Yes, and he's going to do the poem first. Is that okay?"

I tried hard not to glance at Andre or my brother. "That's perfect. Let me start the recording."

COLD JUSTICE PODCAST

Season 4, Episode 4
Behind the Lens - The Friend

Recorded on Saturday, June 14

JOSS: Welcome back to the *Cold Justice Podcast*. I'm Joss Miller. Today I'm speaking with Tre Kennedy, a spoken word artist and close friend of Jerome "Lens" McAbee. Before we get started, Tre is going to share a poem he wrote in memory of Lens.

TRE: *Behind the lens, he walked these streets.*
Not as a collector of things, but of truth.
Each click of the shutter, small rebellion against forgetting.
Some folks didn't like what he chose to remember.
Preferring those stories stayed buried.
But he knew the lens reveals what the heart refuses to see
That painful truths can't stay hidden forever.
We who remain must be the lens now.

We must focus on what matters.

JOSS: Tre, thank you for joining me. What a beautiful tribute to your friend.

TRE: Thanks for having me on, Joss, and I appreciate the feedback. I hope your listeners enjoy my words.

JOSS: I'm sure they will. Lens left many fans of his work. But you were his oldest friend. You two grew up in Atlanta together. Can you tell me about your friendship?

TRE: Man, Lens was my brother from another mother, you know? We both attended a magnet high school that got us interested in the arts early. I was writing and doing spoken word. He was drawing and getting into photography. We used to talk about how we were going to change the world with our art.

JOSS: That's cool that Lens took photos and that he could draw. He must have been so talented.

TRE: Yes, he was! And here's a little known fact about Lens for your listeners. At one time, he wanted to illustrate comic books. He was really good at it, but then he started using a camera and that became his passion.

JOSS: So cool! You know what? From what I can tell, Lens was a hero who didn't wear a cape. Through his camera lens, he gave a voice to people who were often overlooked.

TRE: Yeah, Lens was something special.

JOSS: Now, how did you both end up in Charleston?

TRE: Lens moved to Charleston since he had family here. He was born here but moved to Atlanta with his dad after his parent's divorce. I missed my boy Lens. He seemed to love Charleston more than Atlanta, so I came to visit a few times. There's so much history in this place, both good and bad. I finally moved here about six years ago. But I'm back and forth, traveling to Atlanta and other places with my show.

JOSS: I understand Lens's father, Lance McAbee was killed in Atlanta. That grief might have driven him to be closer to his mother and family.

TRE: [pauses] Yeah, I can agree with that.

JOSS: Let's talk about that Atlanta trip Lens took a few weeks before he died. Were you on that trip with him?

TRE: Yeah, I had a show at this little venue in Midtown. Lens and I drove up together.

JOSS: Others have mentioned he was different after that trip. After talking to his former girlfriend, Zara, she thought he probably visited his father's grave.

TRE: Yeah, that was the main reason for the trip. But he still came out to support my show and hang out with people we knew.

JOSS: I imagine it still hurt him not knowing what happened to his father. Were they close?

TRE: [pauses] Yeah. Lance, we called him L.B., was a pretty cool dude. Lens really loved his Pops. Lens was [long pause] ...He was asking a lot of questions about his father, you know, about what happened that night. He kept bothering the detectives on the case.

JOSS: Seven years is a long time. I imagine the trail had grown cold. Did they give him any information?

TRE: No. They always gave him the runaround. You know how it is. Cops have to move on to new cases.

JOSS: Yeah, it's a shame that some cases go cold. I was looking through Lens's old Instagram posts last night. We talked earlier about Lens's desire to create comic books. Did you know he posted some of his drawings? I really liked the superhero with the lightning bolt symbol across his chest. Do you remember that character?

TRE: [pauses] Yeah. Lens called him "Voltage." Made him shoot lightning out of his arms.

JOSS: The lightning bolt spiraled slightly, giving it movement. Not like the standard comic book style.

TRE: [pauses] Yeah, Lens was always particular about his art.

MAYA: [off-camera, voice low] What does this have to do with Lens's death?

TRE: [lowers voice] Maya, we're recording. Not now.

MAYA: [moving into frame] Wait... [she grabs Tre's arm and pushes up his sleeve] Show her your arm.

TRE: [yanking his arm away, voice going cold] Maya —

MAYA: What? I was showing Joss. You and Lens got matching tattoos in high school, right?

TRE: [turning away from the camera, voice grows louder] You don't know when to leave things alone, like your brother.

MAYA: [voice rising] What? Why are you acting like this?

TRE: [turns to the screen, eyes cold] This interview is over.

MAYA: [screams] No! Tre, you're hurting me!

[Call ends]

Saturday, June 14 at 9:52 p.m.

I jumped up from the couch. My body trembling from Maya's scream right before Tre ended the call. "Oh, my goodness. The tattoo. It's the same as on the pill. That's crazy!"

TYORA MOODY

I looked from Andre to Nate, who were both standing.

"We have to do something." I held my hands to my head. "You should have seen his face. Do you think he knew I was trying to connect him with Len's death? Poor Maya! Wait, Zara and her son are over there too."

I was past the point of freaking out, practically hyperventilating.

Andre grabbed my shoulders. "Joss. Joss. Breathe."

I stared into his eyes. Slowly, I inhaled and exhaled. We did this together for a few minutes. Andre touched my chin. "Are you good?"

I nodded, too afraid to speak. Too scared my thoughts would tumble out again. Tre's eyes... and Maya's scream still reverberated in my head.

"We got this." He looked over at Nate. "I'm going to sound the alarm with Wilkes."

Lens and Tre had the same tattoo. What did that mean?

Andre stood in the kitchen talking on the phone. My brother had called someone on his phone. I grabbed mine from the coffee table and sat on the couch. I pulled up the Instagram app and went to Lens's feed. I studied his last post, his selfie.

I'd noticed he had tattoos, but this time I looked closer.

Within the individual frames of the tattooed filmstrip on Len's bicep was the lightning bolt design. Same as the one on Tre's biceps except his was slightly bigger. Were Lens and Tre in on this together, working to create a pill and distribute it in the community? I didn't want to believe that about Lens. But Andre had mentioned he'd been in trouble before. I didn't know his background.

What I knew was Lens didn't accidentally die that night.

And the man who was supposed to be his oldest friend had been keeping a secret. Why else would he get so agitated about the tattoo?

I didn't think I was being obvious about where I was going, and I wasn't even sure I could bring up the Bolt pill.

Next to me, I felt, rather than saw, someone sit on the couch with me.

It was Nate.

I pointed to the tattoo on Lens's arm. "Have you seen this?"

Nate leaned in. "Joss, just because they both have matching tattoos, doesn't mean Lens was involved. If Tre stole Lens's design for the pills, that would be a reason to keep him quiet."

I gulped. "You mean to kill him? Tre would know that Lens wouldn't go near the water, but maybe that's where they met. Lens saw what was on this pill and knew it wasn't a coincidence.

Maybe they were the only two that had known about the design, getting the tattoo together. But why use it?"

Nate crossed his arms. "From what I've seen in my undercover work, guys like Tre use symbols that mean something to them. It's a power move. He took Lens's creation and turned it into his brand. Every pill sold is like marking his territory."

"But wouldn't that be risky? Using something so traceable?"

Nate sighed. "Tre was probably arrogant enough to think no one would catch on. Plus, the money is a whole other addiction. And with Tre traveling constantly for his 'shows', he had the perfect distribution network underneath his artist tour schedule."

I looked around, noticing Andre had gone. I was on edge, wondering if they would get to Tre, hoping he wouldn't hurt anyone else. I turned back to my brother. "So you think Lens found out that his design had become associated with overdoses and deaths? That might have been why Lens was so upset after Atlanta."

Nate nodded. "He felt responsible. His art was killing people. And he knew the source. There's something else I looked into after listening to your podcast. You brought it up briefly before things went south with Tre."

Anxiety radiated in my chest. "What?"

Nate licked his lips. "You were concerned about Lens's dad. How his murder wasn't solved? Lens's dad was an artist too."

"Yes. You think there's a connection to Lance McAbee's death too?"

"Think about it. Lens grew up with his dad, another artist. Maybe Lance was familiar with his son's artwork? According to research, Bolt started years before it caught on."

I sucked in a breath before giving voice to Nate's theory. "You think Tre could have something to do with Lance's death?"

He eyed me. "It's a possibility. Whoever attacked Lance, he had to have let them into the studio. There was no forced entry like a typical robbery. Whoever killed Lance made it appear like a robbery after the fact."

I rubbed my hand across my face trying to process all this. Andre returned to the living room. "They got him. Wilkes is bringing Tre in. Maya, Zara, and the little boy are safe."

I placed my hands over my chest, heart beating fast from adrenaline.

Thank you, Lord!

Chapter 18
After the Grind

Wednesday, June 18 at 10:35 a.m.

Zara's interview was published on Monday. The episode received a ton of traffic. Tre's arrest had been the talk of several social media accounts during the weekend. Strangely enough, Maya's Instagram feed was silent. Someone she'd been involved with all this time was the person responsible for her brother's death. I was sure the revelation had shaken her.

This time, when Wednesday rolled around, I made sure I took the day off. Or at least I stayed away from the café. There were some things I still needed to wrap up for this season of the *Cold Justice Podcast*. I would eventually release the episode with Tre even though it stopped abruptly.

Andre thought I should sit on it and let things play out in the legal system. From his suggestion, I shared it with Wilkes.

I parked my car near the Sugar Creek Lofts, a historic building where artists still hung out. When I got out, I could hear the sounds of children's laughter at the nearby playground. Zara was sitting on a bench, watching her son play with other children. She wore oversized sunglasses, but removed them when she turned her head toward me. Her eyes were puffy from crying.

"Thanks for meeting me," I said, settling onto the bench beside her.

Zara nodded. "I'm glad you reached out. I've been wanting to say thank you."

"No need. Maya is the one who wanted all this to happen." I paused. "Have you heard from her? She's not answering any of my messages or DMs. Her social media went completely silent."

"She's heartbroken," Zara said quietly. "We all are. Tre was supposed to be Lens's best friend. Finding out he was involved..." She shook her head. "I still can't believe it. You know he gave Devante those pills."

I absorbed this. "What?"

Zara was quiet for a long time. "We talked. Devante and me. We think Tre had been trying to set him up this whole time. Tre had been in Maya's ear, blowing everything out of proportion, making it seem like Devante, Lens, and I had this crazy love triangle."

"I'm really sorry. Tre was good with his words, but he was spinning some other tales."

Zara smirked. "Yeah. There was always something off with Tre, but I couldn't put my finger on it."

"What do you mean?"

She watched her son, who now was climbing up the slide. Once he safely slid down, Zara began speaking again. "Everyone saw him and Lens as these tight friends. But when I started dating Lens, I noticed things. The way Tre made little comments about Lens's follower count. How he'd suggest Lens was trying to be some man of the people with his photography and videos. It felt like... jealousy to me."

I thought back to Tre's performance at Friday Night Jam, about how he'd dedicated his set to Lens. Maya had filmed it. "He seemed genuinely affected by Lens's death."

"Oh, I think he was," Zara said. "That's what makes this so twisted. I think Tre really cared about Lens. But he also resented him."

The pieces were connecting in my mind, forming a picture I didn't like. Did Tre knowingly lead Lens to his death? Did they argue and Lens slipped into the water? Or did Tre push his friend into the water and watch him struggle? Probably listening to his cries for help.

I shook my head. "You said you talked to Devante. How is he?"

She hesitated. "Devante's getting help. He's still facing legal troubles. The lawyer says he could probably get a plea deal since he's cooperating. Since he received the pills directly from Tre, he can help build the case against him."

"I'm glad he's getting help. I hope he can pick his business back up. He's a really good photographer."

"Me too." Zara put her sunglasses back on. "Listen, if Maya doesn't reach out to you, be patient with her. She's a mess right now."

I nodded. "When you talk to her, tell her I'm here if she needs anything. Same for you too, okay."

Zara gave me a genuine smile. "Take care of yourself, Joss. You and your podcast are doing important work. I'm forever grateful that the truth is finally out."

I strode back to my car, my steps feeling lighter.

Two weeks later
Sunday Dinner

The aroma of Mom's roast chicken filled the house, mingling with the scent of fresh rolls from the oven. I couldn't remember the last time my mom hosted Sunday dinner. I finished setting the dining room table with Mom's good dishes. After her adoptive parents died, Mom had selected a few things to keep. The china with the delicate gold trim usually only came out on special occasions.

"Hey, Mom, the table's set and ready to go." I said as I strolled back into the kitchen. "Mmm, everything smells so good in here."

My mom smiled. "I figured it was long past due for me to pull out the pots and pans while Nate was still here. Plus, he's been dropping hints about missing my cooking."

It was good to see Nate and Mom getting along despite the number of ways her baby boy had shocked her with his secret life. No surprise there. Nate always got out of trouble with Mom easier than me.

The doorbell rang, and a few seconds later, I heard Nate's booming voice along with two excited female voices. Aunt Ruth and Aunt Thelma swept into the kitchen, both carrying covered dishes.

"I brought collard greens," Aunt Ruth announced, setting her dish on the kitchen counter.

Aunt Thelma placed her dish beside her sister's. "And I made a peach cobbler for dessert."

"Y'all didn't have to bring anything," Mom protested.

Aunt Ruth said. "Clarice, you know we love to cook. We're happy to contribute. Oh, look. There's Louise."

I'd called mom last night to ask her if it was okay for Louise to come. It seemed mean to leave her out of the Sunday meals.

When we arrived an hour ago, Mom reached down and hugged her biological mother. "Louise, thank you for coming."

Looking shocked and pleased at the same time, my grandmother choked out, "Thank you for inviting me, Clarice."

The relationship between the two women was still a work in progress, but at least Mom was trying.

Andre arrived last, looking handsome in a white button-down shirt and khakis. He gave me a kiss first and then charmed all the women in my family with a peck on the cheek.

Once everyone was seated around the table, Aunt Ruth led us in grace. Her soothing voice thanked the Lord for family, for food, and for second chances. When she said "Amen," we echoed it back and began passing around dishes. For a while, the only sounds were the clinking of silverware and murmurs of appreciation for the meal.

Then Nate cleared his throat. "So, I wanted to let everyone know I'll be heading back to Atlanta next week."

My fork paused halfway to my mouth. I'd known this was coming and wondered if it was really safe for my brother to go back. After Tre's arrest a few weeks ago, Andre told me the spoken word artist cut a deal by dropping some names. Hopefully, the police in Atlanta had caught everyone.

My eyes flitted in Mom's direction. The smile she'd sported most of the afternoon faded.

"My SAC called yesterday," Nate explained. "They've wrapped up the operation. Thanks to some key testimony from... a recent arrest, they were able to dismantle the whole network. The makers of those Bolt pills are all in custody."

"Nate, that's wonderful news about the case," Aunt Thelma said. "It's been so good to get to know you better while you've been visiting."

Nate smiled. "I will visit more often. Can't miss out on all this good home cooking."

Mom eyed him. "I like the sound of that. Even though I still don't like your job, I'm proud of you. Your father would be too."

Nate cleared his throat and looked down at his plate. "Thanks, Mom."

Andre and I insisted on cleaning up the kitchen, so the women congregated in the living room while Nate excused himself to make a phone call. Even though it was my mom's kitchen, Andre and I moved around with ease. I wiped down the countertops while Andre loaded the dishwasher. We moved back and forth in a comfortable silence that I liked. Andre's presence had a way of making me feel warm and fuzzy inside.

Andre touched my arm as I hung the damp dishcloth on the hook to dry. "Want to step outside for some air?"

"Sure."

He slid open the sliding door that led out to the back deck. The late afternoon sun cast golden light across the small yard. Over in the corner sat my dad's beloved gas grill. It'd been sitting covered since my dad died, and I wondered if it would ever be used again.

Andre sat down in one of the wicker chairs Mom had set up across from the grill. There were so many good memories out here from when I was younger. Those memories swirled around me as I sat beside Andre, our shoulders touching.

"This was nice," he said. "Having everyone together like this."

"It was," I agreed. "With everything that's happened, it feels like we're all in a good place."

"That's what I was thinking." Andre turned to face me, taking one of my hands in his. "Joss, I've been thinking a lot lately about what's important. About what I want for my future."

There was something in his tone, in the way he was looking at me, that made my heart beat faster.

He chuckled. "You make me want to be a better detective. A better man."

"Andre—" I started, but he gently squeezed my hand.

"Let me finish," he said softly. "Life is too short to wait for the perfect moment. There's never going to be a time when I'm not dealing with some case or you're not getting caught up in the next season of *Cold Justice Podcast*. I'm happy we can work through your investigations together."

I giggled nervously.

He reached into his pocket.

My breath caught as he pulled out a small velvet box.

"Joss Miller," he said, dropping to one knee, "I love you more than I thought it was possible to love someone. I want to spend the rest of my life supporting you, protecting you when you'll let me, and being amazed by you every single day."

He opened the box to reveal a beautiful round diamond set on a simple platinum band. It was perfect, and it absolutely took my breath away.

"Will you marry me?"

Tears streamed down my face as I nodded. "Yes. Yes! Oh my God, yes!"

Andre stood and slipped the ring onto my finger, then pulled me into a kiss. The house and surrounding yard where I grew up faded away in my mind.

"I love you so much," I whispered.

"I love you too," he said, pulling me closer.

I don't know how long we were standing wrapped in each other's arms, but I heard the sliding door open. I turned to find my mother, grandmother, great-aunts, and brother all peeking out.

Did they all know?

"Did she say yes?" Mom asked, her eyes bright with tears.

"She said yes!" Andre confirmed, keeping his arm around my waist.

There was a collective cheer. Next thing I knew, everyone was hugging us and admiring the ring.

Nate clapped Andre on the back. "Welcome to the family, bro."

The women in my life gathered around me, already chattering about wedding plans.

I caught Andre's eye.

He winked at me.

I knew that whatever came next, we would face it together.

About the Author

Tyora Moody is the author of **Soul-Searching Mysteries,** which includes **cozy mystery, women sleuth mystery,** and **romantic suspense** under the Christian Fiction genre. Her book series include the Eugeena Patterson Mysteries, Joss Miller Mysteries, Lowcountry Secrets, Serena Manchester Mysteries, Reed Family Mysteries, and the Victory Gospel Mysteries.

When Tyora isn't working for a literary client, she's either loving on her cats, listening to an audiobook or podcast, binge-watching crime shows or Marvel movies, and of course, thinking about the next book.

To contact Tyora about reviewing her books or book club discussions, visit her online at TyoraMoody.com.

Join her newsletter at https://tyoramoody.substack.com/

Tyora Moody's Books

Eugeena Patterson Mysteries

Deep Fried Trouble, #1

Oven Baked Secrets, #2

Lemon Filled Disaster, #3

A Simmering Dilemma, #4

An Unsavory Mess, #5

A Spicy Predicament, #6

Marinated Conditions, #7

Eugeena Patterson Family Shorts

Shattered Dreams, #1

A Blended Family Christmas, #2

Falling in Love... Again!, #3

Joss Miller Mysteries
Double Mocha Blues, #1
A Latte Mayhem, #2
Mint-Flavored Trouble, #3
Steamy Espresso Secrets, #4

Serena Manchester Mysteries
Hostile Eyewitness, prequel
Bittersweet Motives, #1
Dangerous Confessions, #2
Waning Innocence, #3
Presumed Guilty, #4
Shifting Blame, #5

Lowcountry Secrets (Romantic Suspense)
The Homecoming, #1
The Reckoning, #2

Reed Family Mysteries
Broken Heart, #1
Troubled Heart, #2
Relentless Heart, #3
With All My Heart, #3.5

Faithful Heart, #4
Wounded Heart, #5

Victory Gospel Series (Mysteries)
When Rain Falls, #1
When Memories Fade, #2
When Perfection Fails, #3

Victory Gospel Shorts (Sweet Romance)
The Replacement Date, #1
Southern Delights, #2
When Love Finds Me, #3
Nobody's Replacement, #4
A Southern Delights Christmas, #5
Holding on to Love, #6

www.ingramcontent.com/pod-product-compliance
Lightning Source LLC
Chambersburg PA
CBHW070839250626
47159CB00003B/853